The Kinda Fella I Am

Advance Praise
for THE KINDA FELLA I AM

"Raymond Luczak's *The Kinda Fella I Am* presents readers with the most diverse tapestry of characters in contemporary queer literature. From the gay wheelchair user reflecting back on his life as he cruises men at a leather bar to the self-described confirmed masturbator critiquing the ableism of the radical faeries, the amazing array of 'fellas' in Luczak's stories are fierce, fabulous, and filled with desire. No other collection of stories maps the rich intersections of queer, Deaf, and disabled cultures like *The Kinda Fella I Am*."

—Robert McRuer, author of *Crip Theory: Cultural Signs of Queerness and Disability* and co-editor of *Sex and Disability*

"Raymond Luczak's narrators tell their stories with voices brimming with pride, rage, and hope. Their experiences rise from the page like wildfire, ferocious and breathtaking, burning away our preconceptions of disability and leaving us dazzled."

—Michael Thomas Ford, author of *Lily*

"This book is obscene, tender, queer, innovative, and very disabled. This book will turn you on."

—Jillian Weise, author of *The Amputee's Guide to Sex*

"These fifteen accessible, and entertaining, eyewitness stories of physical identity and existential inequities are 'performance-art arias' of desire, anxiety, and hope capable of rocking the consciousness of even the most sympathetic readers curious about the hazards to all that are inherent in gay society's quarantine of people labeled disabled."

—Jack Fritscher, PhD, author of *Mapplethorpe: Assault* and *Gay San Francisco*

The Kinda Fella I Am
Stories

Raymond Luczak

Scott —
you're my
kinda fella!
Hugs
2/20/18

RECLAMATION PRESS
Berkeley, California

In Gratitude

The author is forever grateful to those who've guided these stories and hence this book in one form or another: Jane Berliss-Vincent, Matthew Bright, Russell Bunge, Louis Flint Ceci, David Cummer, Arthur Durkee, Michael Thomas Ford, Jack Fritscher, Bambi Gauthier, Ibby Grace, James C. Johnstone, Ian Markauskas, Robert McRuer, Chael Needle, Corbett Joan OToole, Sam Schmitt, Kristal Sierra, Christopher Smith, Tom Steele, Carter Lynn Thurmond, Jillian Weise, and Cynthia Weitzel.

Disclaimer

This is a work of fiction. Names, characters, businesses, places, events, and incidents are either the products of the author's imagination or used in a fictitious manner.

Copyright

Stories

Acknowledgments

The following stories, some of which have been revised, appeared in these journals and anthologies.

All in Your Head: "My Line of Feeling."
Art & Understanding: "The Heaven of Our Eyes" (incorporated into "The Room of My Eyes").
Exposure: "A Crip Fairy Tale."
Eyes of Desire: A Deaf Gay & Lesbian Reader (Raymond Luczak, ed.; Alyson): "You Feel Beautiful."
The Gambler: "Lazarus."
Guide to Kulchur Creative Journal: "Night Latitudes."
The Myriad Carnival: Queer and Weird Stories from Under the Big Top (Matthew Bright, ed.; Lethe Press): "September Song."
Not Just Another Pretty Face (Louis Flint Ceci, ed.; Beautiful Dreamer Press): "Kicks."
Quickies 3: Short Short Fiction on Gay Male Desire (James C. Johnstone, ed.; Arsenal Pulp Press): "The Room of My Eyes."
RFD Magazine: "Community Building."

"This" was adapted from the play *This*. The author thanks Christopher Smith for entrusting him with its initial story. He also thanks Fred Michael Beam for producing and directing its initial production with Christopher Smith and Warren "Wawa" Snipe/Kriston Lee Pumphrey, respectively, on January 10/11, 2003 at Gallaudet University. The story is in memory of Cagney S. Perkins (1961-1991) and William D. Byrd (1966-1993).

The story "Lazarus" is in memory of Cook Friedman (1949-1993).

"A Crip Fairy Tale" is in honor of Christopher Hewitt (1946-2004).

"The Room of My Eyes" is in memory of the author's 25 Deaf friends and acquaintances who've died from AIDS-related complications.

The Kinda Fella I Am

When I show up at the Eagle, I scare the shit out of strangers. There's the mud-splattered spokes of my wheels, the beat-up edges of my seat, the crud-smoothed-over bike bar handles behind my shoulders. You could say this older chair's my Harley-Davidson. I got on my t-shirt and leather vest, and my jeans folded underneath my stumps. I got two nice cigars packed inside my vest. Once my buddy Artie brings me my beer, I'll have settled out here in the smoking patio where other guys smoke their cigars and shoot the breeze. I like the way my leather cap fits on my head. It's a nice feeling.

But tonight is different. I've caught you standing by the wall with your buddies, drinking and talking even in the din of music blaring. You're in your thirties. Cute smile. Sharp flattop. Nice ass.

Repeat: *nice* ass.

Oh, yeah. I'm gonna snooker you before the night's over. You just don't know it yet.

Now, I didn't use to think this way about anybody. I used to be the kinda fella who was expected to sit quietly in his wheelchair by the sidelines; better if I never showed up at all. I've been disabled since I was nine years old. My parents died in a car accident, but lucky me, I wore my seatbelt in the back. It took me months to get used to moving around. The pains were the worst. I had really bad nightmares about riding in a car again. You should know that before the accident, I was one of those overly active boys who loved to climb trees, shoot rocks with my slingshot, and stuff, and then—bam! I'd never thought anything about wheelchairs until the day I woke up with the worst headache in the world. I didn't feel right in the head, but I didn't have the words back then to describe it. I knew I wasn't right, and it had nothing to do with my legs being amputated. The reality of my legs slowly dawned on me, and that's when I got so pissed-off at the world. Everyone was surprised at the foul language I spewed out. They'd thought that because I was still a boy, I didn't know shit about expressing my rage in adult language. They quarantined me in a private room until they felt I wouldn't swear my head off. Then I was brought back to this big room where six of us boys slept. The other boys had mobility problems, but none of them were amputees. I learned later that many people who lose the use of their limbs in accidents like mine often have episodes of PTSD. Their thinking processes skip a step now and then. That's me. It's not so bad anymore. I have a driver's license, and I own a car with hand controls.

But for a long time many people didn't think that kids could have PTSD. They thought it was strictly for soldiers who came back home. They said that since I hadn't fought in a war, I had to toughen up and get with the program. So I did. Or so I thought.

Over time I became a very good boy. Hard to believe when you look at me now, but it's true.

Aunt June and Uncle Tim, having heard from my parents all along what a difficult child I was, were surprised to find me meek and obedient by the time I realized I had to live with them in St. Louis. When I left the hospital, I was already doing my homework on time so I wasn't behind grades-wise. I read books. I watched television without demanding to see my favorite shows. I felt that God was punishing me for having been an unruly boy. He was telling me that I had to shape up or I'd lose my arms next.

Living with Aunt June and Uncle Tim was hard. Even before the accident, I'd never liked them much. They always struck me as a bit haughty, and they weren't poor at all. I didn't like my cousins either. Tom and Terry thought my little wheelchair was freakish. They had seen adult-sized wheelchairs, but they'd never seen a kid-sized chair before. I slept in a tiny room that used to be the pantry behind the kitchen because there was no other place for me on the first floor. They ripped out the shelves and wallpapered it and put in a twin-sized mattress. They found a bedframe with drawers below it because there was no room for a closet. They put in a reading lamp above my bed, and that was it. My door was just a curtain, so I didn't have any real privacy. I also had the tiniest room of anyone in that house. They expanded the first floor bathroom for me with the money I'd inherited from my parents; Aunt June and Uncle Tim had to fight my attorney hard to release some of that money for the bathroom renovation.

No one was supposed to touch that money until I was eighteen. I know I shouldn't complain about my aunt and uncle's generosity, but I felt worse than an orphan. Seeing that I wasn't equal to anyone, not even my own relatives, really hurt. I know, I know. I shouldn't complain, but *damn*. Even though I'd seen the upstairs and the attic when I visited them before the accident, I never saw upstairs again once I moved in with Aunt June and Uncle Tim. It was as if the able-bodied moved about in a world of their own, emitting their footsteps and laughs muffled through the ceiling. They belonged to the heavens, and I didn't. At the dinner table I sat at one end; at times it felt as if they didn't want me any closer.

I learned to perfect my poker face. I was a tough little boy who did very well at school. That shocked everyone who'd known me before the accident. I had never liked books. Took me a long time to see that books weren't so bad. They kept me company when my cousins went off to do events where I couldn't participate, like at the waterslide park or the amusement rides. Every time I heard them break out in squeals and laughs, I wanted to bash their heads in. Their freedom of joyful motion reminded me of the very thing denied to me.

I began having fantasies of having wings like an angel, but painted with a crimson red like the Devil. I'd carry a baseball bat and swoop down on anyone who didn't try to figure out how to include people like me. I'd just bop off their heads like the Queen of Hearts demanded in *Alice in Wonderland*. Their deaths would be just punishment. Anyone who says, "I'm so sorry you can't join us," with a pout after not even investigating other options, deserves to be shot. Nobody ever looks you in the eye and tells you how sexy you are. Nobody asks you out on a date. You're worse than a nobody. The very things designed to carry us through life are the very things that repel everyone. I'm always shocked that more disabled people haven't shot able-bodied people. Humiliation happens to be a hallmark of ableism. But I didn't know the language of disability back then.

See? I'm still here. While I talk with Artie and his buddies, I'm noticing how you've been glancing back at me. You think you've played this game before, but I've learned to play the game differently.

In St. Louis, I went to elementary school. I hated every moment of it, especially during the elementary school graduation ceremony. They had planks ready for me to go onto the makeshift stage, but they wouldn't put them there until the very end. Didn't matter that my last name begins with a K. "You understand, right?" wasn't even a question when they told me how I'd come up at the end of the roll call.

For my high school graduation, I had to wait backstage. There were no ramps from the audience onto the stage itself, and so my aunt and uncle waited with everyone else. I was alone backstage, listening to everyone clap and cheer as they received their diplomas. At least I wasn't saved until the end, as in "saving the best for last," which was how someone had jokingly put it. When my turn came, I wheeled onstage. As Principal Roysen handed me my diploma, I heard applause, which was louder than usual. Parents were standing with a few tears trickling down their cheeks, and my classmates were dutifully clapping with them. Sure, I had a 4.0 GPA, but I knew why they were applauding. They were telling themselves what an inspiration I was, that I'd conquered my stumps to score a perfect 4.0, but you know what? If I hadn't lost my legs, I'd have dropped out of school a long time before. I've always had this streak of meanness, and ever since God punished me, well ... I had to be a good boy. I didn't have a choice.

Onstage, I wanted so much to show them my middle finger, but I didn't. I should've. It's one of my biggest regrets. What did they know of my life? Nothing. I was only inspiration porn in action: an ordinary guy doing something that any able-bodied person did as a matter of course and yet because he had no legs, it was somehow deemed an extraordinary act. Wow. Look at him! Isn't he amazing? With inspiration porn, you don't ejaculate; you expel tears of gratitude and click on "Share" on Facebook.

No thank you.

When I went to college, I didn't know what I wanted to study. I'd gotten a full four-year scholarship to the University of California in Berkeley. The first day of my New Student Orientation shocked the hell out of me. I had gotten there early because I've learned to expect time-consuming delays getting to a new place. If the elevator isn't working, I'd have to use the freight elevator or wait for someone to show up with the chairlift key. A few students had drifted into the hallway. A perky woman with a bright orange perm came up to me. "You're Alan Kresnick, right?"

"Yes."

"Hi. I'm Sarah Oswald from the Disability Support Services here. You should know that we provide not only support services but also disability-friendly social events so you don't have to feel like a freak around here." She stopped herself. "Sorry. I shouldn't have said that. That was so unprofessional of me."

"No, it's okay," I said.

She had me at the word "freak." How was it possible for an able-bodied person to understand me in a non-patronizing way? No one had ever tried.

4

It was the first time that I began to like the word "freak."

I didn't know what to expect at my first Disability Dance on campus that second Friday in September. I'd spotted a few wheelchair users here and there, but I always averted my eyes. I was too ashamed to be counted in their company. I'd somehow been raised to look at other disabled people as lesser than me. By then I'd learned my way around campus—elevators, classrooms, the whole enchilada. When I saw that my new room had its own accessible bathroom, I nearly cried. Imagine, at the age of 18, finally having a room of your own, with a *real* door and a *real* bathroom designed to be accessible in the first place. Oh, how I loved that room! It was the first time I'd felt at home after my accident. I knew I couldn't go back to St. Louis again. Now that I'd come of age, Aunt June and Uncle Tim dropped occasional hints about my lending them money so they could renovate their house for sale. When I saw my new room for the first time, I realized how little they'd done for me. Everything they'd done for me was just a favor.

As long as I had my own room, I was very happy. Quite excited, actually, to go to classes. That was another thing I'd learned. College students are a markedly different breed from high schoolers; they were at least respectful of me. They didn't cluster into cliques and whisper about me; they didn't have time to linger. They had the next class, the next assignment, the next reading to contend with. I had been pretty much alone so that was fine by me, but my first Disability Dance changed everything.

I didn't show up on time. I was afraid of being the only one there, making my loneliness transparent. That was the first time I'd grasped why people didn't like to show up on time for parties. A petite woman with a buzzcut seemed to be the deejay with her CD player setup. She was playing the Tears for Fears's "Sowing the Seeds of Love." I'd heard the song before, but I'll always link it to the memory of seeing all sorts of people in wheelchairs, leg braces, and neck braces. I wanted to mock them for looking so lame with their outfits. They weren't going to look cool no matter how hard they tried. I didn't dare look into their eyes as they carried on, laughing. They were worse off than me, and they were having a good time? How dare they! I was better than them. The dance took place in an oversized conference room with tables pushed to the wall, and its chairs were spaced quite a few feet apart. I thought that was an odd configuration until I realized that was for the benefit of wheelchair users and able-bodied people who wanted to sit next to them and watch others dancing. The lights weren't even dimmed.

And the dancing itself? I cringed from watching. These freaks couldn't keep in sync with the music. It was all so dorky. Were we supposed to applaud such heroic efforts at dancing? No. I thought of spinning around and leaving, but I caught a hand waving out of the corner of my eye.

A stubby man with a beard and a leg brace smiled at me. I'd never noticed him before. He sat off to the side. I glanced both ways as if I were about to cross the street and wheeled over to him.

"You already hate it here," he said. "You think you're better than us."

I gasped. "How did you know?"

"It's obvious. Plus I've been here three years so I know all the cripples here. Except you and two other guys. I'm hoping they'll come here tonight."

"Oh."

"You don't have to say anything. I'm Kerry."

We shook hands. I looked at his hand and then at him.

"What's wrong?"

"It's ... it's weird, but this is the first time I've shaken hands with a ... disabled guy."

"You serious?"

I shook my head no. "Weird, huh?"

"No, it's not."

Kerry and I talked and talked that night. I knew by the time the dance was over, I was in love with him. Didn't matter that he was straight, or that he was open-minded enough to accept my compliments. He had a way of bringing me out. All it took was one question. "I know it's not really my business, but are you gay? It's just that you made me wish I were gay, but I'm not. You're a really nice guy."

I nodded, and he did the very best thing a friend could do for me. He took my hands and held them without an iota of fear. "Great. Do you want me to introduce you to some gay guys here?"

"Wait. There are—there are disabled gay guys?"

"Oh, come off it. You can't be the only studmuffin around here."

I laughed. No one had ever called me that.

You see why I was so in love with Kerry Wright? I wanted him in the worst way. He was funny, kind, smart, and not homophobic at all. He was also the one who said, "You need to know the history of your people."

"People? I have no people."

He pointed to the crips dancing and talking. "They've put up with as much crap as you have. Yeah, I'd say they're your people."

That night I made a lot of new friends, but my main ones turned out to be Phil, Mark, Roddy, and Miguel. We became the Five Musketeers of a sort. It was scary at first to see that these guys, so different from each other and yet similar to me, could be into guys.

We five got together every weekend, and I learned not to care anymore what others thought of us. Like Phil said, "We've spent all our time trying to kiss their asses, and you know what? It hasn't worked. I say, Fuck 'em if they can't deal with freaks like us. We are freaks, crips, fags, whatever."

Is it possible to be in love with five different guys at the same time? I know I was. I cared intensely for each one of them in my own way.

Phil had grown up using forearm crutches for his cerebral palsy in Los Angeles; his father was a producer at a major studio. He rarely saw him as he was always working on location or hustling for his next production deal. His mother looked after Phil and his three other siblings. She was fiercely loyal to him that when she divorced her husband, she insisted on keeping Phil. "That man doesn't care about you or anyone but himself," she said. "One day you're gonna meet a special girl." She wasn't upset at all when he told her that he was attracted to the Fed Ex guy who showed up every other day up at their house. She simply changed her tune to, "One day you're gonna meet a special guy. I can't wait to meet him!" All of us wanted Phil's mother to be our mother. She was still active in fundraising for CP research.

Mark initially had good vision but as he entered his adolescence, his vision dropped steadily until he realized that his retinitis pigmentosa was indeed for real. His family had a genetic predisposition for RP, so his tunnel vision with no peripheral view was no big surprise. It was funny that, while he was growing up, he didn't feel like he fit in with his blind father and uncles until he himself couldn't see very well. "Welcome to the club," they said. "We'll tell you all our secrets." Away from their sighted relatives, they shared dirty jokes, usually involving naked women and canes. He was initially upset about being blind, but his father, who was a sound engineer for symphony recordings, took him aside. "You just have to live differently. It's not better or worse. Just different." Mark didn't come out to his parents until he was twenty-one. It wasn't easy for them to come around, but they did. Mark was a senior majoring in engineering; he was interested in developing voice-directed technology.

Then there was Roddy. He was a little person in a powered wheelchair. He had the head of an adult man, but his body seemed smooth and soft as a baby's. Of all the disabled guys I'd met, he took some getting used to. I didn't want to stare at the strangeness of his body. He had a wonderful laugh. I was grateful that he hadn't pointed out my sense of unease around him. He wanted to be an artist like his idol Henri de Toulouse-Lautrec. He had no interest in creating dour-faced disability art; he wanted sparkle and pizzazz in his work.

Later, when it was time for all of us to leave the Disability Dance, Kerry said, "Congratulations. You're one of the cool people now."

"What?"

"The way you tried not to look at Roddy is exactly how cool people try not to look at you."

His observation hit me hard. I'd long sworn never to gawk at anyone.

"It's okay," he said. "Just hug him when you see him the next time. He'll know you're not afraid of him."

And Miguel? He had grown up in Oakland, the next town over from Berkeley. He'd grown up speaking both Spanish and English, and he was majoring in Chinese with a minor in business administration. He wanted to become an interpreter for corporations wanting to do business with China. He had a huge burn scar on one side of his face; if you saw him on that side for the first time, you'd be horrified, but if you saw him on the good side for the first time, you'd think, Wow, what a sexy man. He'd a number of surgeries done to his face. He had been a member of gangs all his life until that day when a stranger tossed a lidless paint can full of acid at his face. That was when he realized that gangs weren't for him anymore. Too much fighting, too much tension. He was built. He was the kinda guy no one would believe to be gay, but he was. He wasn't technically disabled, but we freaks and crips never treated him like an outcast. When we Five Musketeers went out together, he became something of a safety net for Phil when he tried to hurry up with the rest of us. Miguel was usually quiet, but of all my friends, he and I had the most intensely philosophical conversations about what it meant to be different. He was the one who said I should think about becoming an attorney. I went into pre-law.

These guys were like family to me. It felt so good to talk honestly about our attraction to men, and even better when we talked about lookism and ableism. By then I had been doing a lot of reading. It was as if a lotus deep inside me had opened up, and it was a whole new world. I loved it. I loved how so many of us were able to come together as a community. It felt like a family reunion at times.

Until I became politically aware, I'd worn prosthetic legs as a matter of habit. I have very short stumps, and they weren't of much help to me; more of a hindrance, really. The only time they were good for was when I needed something to pivot on from chair to toilet, but that depended on how accessible the bathroom was. Alone, I preferred to leave them off. When Kerry came to visit me, he said, "You know, you look much better without those legs. It means you're not trying to be like an able-bodied person."

It was really a scary moment when I put on my pants, folded them under my stumps, and wheeled out to the elevator. Kerry said, "You'll be fine." A few dorm residents, having seen me many times, did a double take in the elevator, but they didn't say anything.

Of course, questions floated across the faces of those familiar strangers walking past on the sidewalk, but no one asked me anything.

Then Kerry had to go back to his place and finish a term paper.

I decided to wheel around downtown Berkeley for the hell of it. The buildings, the cars, the people—well, it was a joy. The sun was shining. No one cared whether I was a freak or not. I was just a stranger who happened to be in a wheelchair. Anonymity can be so liberating.

You know why I'm so tough, so strong now? You have to be if you constantly hear and see how no one wants you as you are. Society says that a man cannot be powerful unless he has two functional legs, or he can't stand and lead. Society says that a man cannot be virile unless he has two functional legs, or he can't fuck. Society says that a man cannot be taken seriously unless he has a fully functional body. Society just won't shut the fuck up! Any crip who breaks through that din is a true warrior. Able-bodied guys will never know the true meaning of warriorhood until they've spent a lifetime with a disability. My boy, you are looking at a kick-ass warrior here. See my fingers here? They're constantly pushing along my wheels to get to where I need to go, but if you ever take off my bike gloves, you'd see that my palms are soft, smooth.

After that sun-soaked afternoon in Berkeley, I decided that in the able-bodied world, I'd continue wearing my prosthetics but at disability events, I'd leave my legs home. But I find that the older I become, the more I prefer to go without my legs. It's my way of saying I have a choice in presenting myself to the world, and no one gets to make that choice for me. I had learned to disregard the societal script that people were supposed to follow once they were found to be disabled. No more. I would not allow myself to be used as an excuse to "inspire" able-bodied people feeling crappy about their own lives. I had to stop pretending that I was that tough little soldier.

My friends—oh, the wonderful gimps and crips and weirdos—thought I was cool. They were gay and straight and lesbian and bisexual, and a few straight women even called themselves queer as a show of solidarity.

They never asked about my stumps or whether I could feel anything down there. They never made a big deal about removing a chair from the table for me when I showed up. That someone would do it automatically for a wheelchair user was a given. They didn't say things like, "Oh, you don't want to dance." It was so exhilarating when us Five Musketeers had decided to storm a bar off the Castro and hug each other, just to show them that we were as "normal" as they were.

We knew what to expect.

We would get thrown out.

But we would call the *San Francisco Chronicle* and the *Bay Area Reporter* and tell them all about it. Shake people up into seeing us as us, not as cripples with braces and canes and wheelchairs, but as human beings like anyone else. No more ignoring us crips as if we were adorable March of Dimes poster children gone ungainly and amok. Jerry Lewis might as well rim our telethon asses.

Everyone would be horrified by our own brand of queer activism and then realize how exclusionary they'd been all along.

It didn't pan out the way we'd hoped.

We lost our nerve when we pushed our way into the bar. We hadn't quite anticipated the difficulty of navigating the dark space amidst the overly loud music. Our ears hurt. And it was dark, too. The bar was packed.

We looked at each other and suddenly felt stupid. What the hell were we doing there? It was their turf, and even if we did make out, it wasn't going to change the fact that it was *still* their turf. They weren't going to learn a thing. They'd get drunk and forget about us, and none of us would go home with anyone. We were worse than the alcoholic dregs who lingered around the bar's closing hour. So humiliating.

We left.

We regrouped in a coffeehouse nearby, and we didn't care whether anyone overheard us. We just lashed out our frustrations, and we cried. The time for shame had long passed. We gripped each other's hands and hugged each other.

Then I had the wildest idea. "Maybe we need to get political with sex."

"Huh? What do you mean?"

"We should have our own queer crip orgy. Have sex with each other."

I was just as shocked as they were at the very notion. I didn't know where *that* came from.

What was stranger, but not really in hindsight, was how we each stared at the tables in front of us and tried not to cry.

It was then I knew I had to do something about it. I was also a virgin.

A few nights later five of us showed up at my friend David's apartment where there was a huge living room overlooking the bay. David was an able-bodied activist who'd worked in homecare for a number of years, and he was very active in the leather and BDSM community. He was known as Sir David, and he brought along two of his slaves, who were ordered to strip naked. It was clear on their faces that they didn't know what to expect after looking at all of us sitting in a half-circle. David ordered them to set up a sling in one end of his living room. It was such a treat for us to watch their lithe bodies—up close and naked!—as they twisted the bars and hooked the chains for the sling. Then they stood with their heads bowed. I found the idea of having able-bodied guys serving us cripples so—*erotic*. That was an exchange of power I hadn't anticipated. David asked us what we needed from him and his slaves, and we took turns to describe our needs. Since Phil had CP, he needed to be held up as the sofa had a very low back. David ordered boy eric to bring a tall-backed chair from the dining room and set it next to the sofa, and boy eric would be responsible for Phil's safety. Mark, not being able to see well at night, asked to be guided around the room so he knew where everyone was before he was led back to his place on the sofa. David assigned boy dale to Mark and explained that boy dale had to describe quietly what the other guys were doing so that Mark would feel included in the group. Roddy was in his chair, and Miguel sat on the far end of the sofa next to Mark. I sat near Phil on the sofa.

Watching David in action, I came to adore him even more. People might think he looked ugly with his acne-scarred face, but I thought he was sexy as hell. Anyone who was willing to lend his apartment for an orgy of gay crips with different needs is a friend in my book. He was nice enough to leave the music's volume and the lights low. He took off his clothes and turned to us. "Anything else, studs? Remember, we're here to do your bidding. No need to be ashamed about trying anything different. Kink is great. Remember, no judging each other. We're all different, and that's what makes all of us great. So, how do you want to get your rocks off?"

I turned to my friends. "Well, I think we need to take our clothes off."

We all laughed nervously.

But taking our clothes off was not the easiest thing in the world. I'd long hated the way my stumps looked. They represented me, and therefore I was ugly as nails hammered into a telephone pole.

We took the longest time to disrobe; sometimes we needed help. Fear quivered in the core of our nakedness.

I was scared. Just what the hell was I doing?

I hadn't anticipated how much harder it would be to look at my crip friends naked. Their bodies were more bony, more mangled than I'd expected, and I felt like the first surge of vomit begin rising in my throat. I squelched it, and I sputtered, "Fuck, dammit. I'm tired of feeling ugly like a barrel of pus." I wanted to cry right there, but I forced myself to continue. "But you know what? I got a ... *dick* here. Yes, I got a dick right here. Just look at this. Yeah. Look at this. My fucking cock. I'm lonely. I'm tired of feeling horny alone all the time. I've never done it with a guy, and I'm fucking nineteen years old!"

I massaged myself, willing myself to get hard. Not easy, but I had to. I didn't want to look into their faces. Too scary.

Yet the most frightening thing I'd ever done in public turned out to be the most liberating thing I've ever done. I realized I had to stop looking at them as if they were undesirable. Sure, we were all friends, but physical imperfection as a deterrent to sexual attractiveness had been so deeply ingrained in us from day one of our births that when we did see each other completely naked apart from our braces and chairs and shoes, we didn't get hard at first. We had become freaks uncaged in a zoo. It was also surreal to hear boy dale try to describe specific details about our bodies into Mark's ear as Mark slowly masturbated in front of us. But I managed to get hard. I was at the center of their freak show, and I didn't want to be the only one. Phil had a small dick, and I couldn't stop looking at it. I kept thinking how I had to make love to these guys as if they're able-bodied. So I pushed myself along the sofa and went down on Phil's cock without warning. He shook and shook in ecstasy while boy eric held him in place so he wouldn't fall off the chair. Then I felt Mark's hands grope all over my body as I continued my sucking. I froze when his fingers roamed all over my naked stumps, but when Mark said, "Wow—feels really nice," I almost cried.

I went back to Phil's cock, my very first cock, and he tasted wonderful. Better than I'd ever imagined! Salty and sweet at the same time. I couldn't get enough of him, even after he came. Crips have the sweetest dicks. I became a confirmed cocksucker that night. I sucked off every man there.

David and his slaves helped us rotate our bodies around the room. I got so turned on by the ferocity of their erections as they watched us freaks do the nasty with each other. The slaves held me up as I fucked my first man in the sling. It was so freeing to stop thinking about waiting for the perfect guy to show up in my doorway, smiling. I like crip cock. Hell, I like *any* cock. Doesn't matter if they get hard or not; big or small, I like them all. It's the guys behind their dicks that turn me on.

Afterwards, David and his slaves spread out sheets on the carpet and arranged pillows for our heads. Sir David said that if he was going to order us crips at all, we should get into the habit of cuddling each other. The only rule was that we couldn't touch each other's dicks. Holding each other, taking turns to explore each other with our fingers, nuzzling, I discovered how amazing and wonderful it was to touch and to be touched without that slight withdrawal of embarrassment. Who knew that Phil's gnarly limbs could feel so wonderful? Or how gentle yet precise Mark's hands could be all over my back? I suddenly envied the Braille-embossed books he'd lugged around. Or the intensely sweet dampness of Roddy's armpits as boy dale held Roddy's legs up. I couldn't stop rubbing my fingers all over Miguel's massive muscles. And so on. I had found my own Garden of Eden. I had no idea that crip guys could be so hot!

Cuddling is what I love most. You have no idea how able-bodied people don't like to touch us, so being touched and held close to another human being is a gift. I think some of us cried when Sir David said that it was already past three o'clock in the morning. We didn't want to let go of each other, but the slaves needed to go home.

Now, I'm looking at you and drinking my beer and wondering if you'd feel repulsed at the idea of us freaks having such an orgy. If so, good! Nobody has that right to dictate what is beautiful for anyone anymore. Those days are over. Ignore the shit that corporations and advertisers want you to believe. They're in the business of making money off your body shame. They want you to feel ugly, so much to the point that you give them billions of dollars as a token of thanks. That way they can feel better with beautiful profits.

Even though us friends didn't have an orgy again, it changed us. We were now crips with benefits. We took turns having sex with each other and did lots of cuddling afterwards. We read *The Joy of Gay Sex* and discovered that disability got a scant mention. Roddy and Mark fell in love and moved in together, and I was so envious of them. I was happy that they still wanted sex with me. It was so empowering to talk about the things that no able-bodied person wanted to hear. Nobody had wanted to hear how frustrated I was from feeling unattractive or how horny I was. I wanted a boyfriend badly, but my crips with benefits were the next best thing. It was great to experiment and practice. You could say that I became a slut. Nobody had wanted to touch me, and now I was. Big time!

Much to my joy, I found a boyfriend. Met him online. Warren was able-bodied. He worked at a bank downtown. My stumps didn't bother him. He had a fetish for amputees. That weirded me out at first, but okay, I thought, if that's what it took to keep a boyfriend, I didn't mind it too much. After one year, though, it started to bother me a great deal. He couldn't stop touching and licking all over my stumps. It was as if I wasn't a person to him anymore. I was just a fetish sex toy. I didn't want to break it off, but I had to. He was very upset, but last I heard, he found another amputee. They're still together as far as I know.

Then I met a really nice guy named Sean in one of my pre-law classes. He wasn't a disability devotee, but we had a great time laughing and carrying on after classes all semester long that one night it just happened in my room. He was honest about my stumps—he wasn't sure if he liked them. I told him that I wasn't sure if I liked them either. That put him at ease. He finally got used to looking at my stumps as if they were just another part of me.

How I loved that man! Damn. He was so sweet, so smart. Oh, he was so cute, too!

But Sean decided to go back to his ex when his asshole ex moved back from Seattle. That was hard. Very hard. I can't convey how fucking painful that felt, being dumped for someone able-bodied. Sean kept saying that wasn't the case, but somehow I think he took the long-range view of us and realized he didn't want a lifetime of having to think constantly about whether a place was accessible before taking me there. I know that if his ex hadn't returned to San Francisco, we'd still be together today.

I graduated second in class with a degree in law. I was excited when I got all those interviews from a few major firms, but I could tell that they lost interest when they saw my chair. Didn't matter that I was salutatorian of my class, or that I scored in mock trials! I loved cross-examination because it was my way of asking the world: why are you still treating me this way? I tried not to be bitter when I saw some classmates who hadn't done as well academically get job offers at big firms. When two able-bodied friends from law school moved to Minneapolis and started up a new law practice, they were aghast to learn that I hadn't gotten a single offer. They had seen my mock trials, so they immediately offered me a spot in their office. They'd grown up there so they knew a lot of potential clients. We all three passed the state bar exam, and before we knew it, we were working way too many hours. But seeing my last name on the plate fronting the reception area—SAMPSON HERNANDEZ KRESNICK, ESQ.—always makes me happy each morning when I come in to work. I make six figures a year, and I live in a house that fits me perfectly so it's easy to cook a nice meal or go to the bathroom. I've had a few boyfriends over the years, but none of them wanted a LTR. No matter—I know I'm a quality catch.

If I'm not too wiped out from work by Friday night, I get ready for the Eagle. I take off my suit and put on my t-shirt. I change over from my high-end wheelchair that I use at the office to my battered chair. I roll up my sleeves to show off my biceps. I'm no different from any of those leather guys who work out and show off their chests in harness. I may not have the legs, but damn, I sure got these beefy arms and powerful hands. I work out, too. See? If I stood up on legs, anyone would see that I got wide shoulders and thick arms. But no, they see only the chair. They maintain a respectful distance. I'm off-limits.

Does it bother me? Nah, because I've got buddies who know me now. Took a while for them to overcome their initial queasiness about me, but you know what? I love the leather and BDSM community. They're more accepting of guys like me because they know what it feels like to be different with their non-mainstream interests. They say hello to me, and we catch up on stuff. It's the strangers who've never met me that are the problem.

Fuck 'em is what I say. They don't know what they're missing.

What are they missing? I'll tell you, my boy.

Are you still looking back at me? Yes, you are.

I'm not a soldier anymore, but I've been to battle and back. I've seen what it takes to build one's own self-confidence. Nobody tells you this, but if you exude self-confidence, someone is gonna sit up and take notice. There isn't enough self-confidence in this world, and that's just like the sexiest thing in the world. Most people don't feel good about themselves, and they want to be around people who do.

Now, that's not the only thing I've learned.

There's no such thing as "they." Guys like you have to stop being "they" long enough to say hello to guys like me. Until then I'm gonna nurse my beer, cross my arms now and then to flex my biceps, and adjust the denim covering my crotch so you can see the outline of my bull balls. I'll light up another cigar and hide myself in a column of smoke so you'd ponder the mystery of this daddy gazing your way. Oh, you're gonna waffle all evening long while you talk with your buddies with occasional glances my way. You'll take lots of bathroom breaks since beer will do that to you, and on the way there and back, you won't be able to take your eyes off me. Your face will be full of questions too embarrassing to voice out loud.

15

My eyes on you will stay steady like an owl's; soon my wheels are going to disappear from the vision that is me, the built-like-a-shithouse daddy who'll strike you as the hottest man you've ever seen. When I catch in your eyes the familiar hesitation about guys like me, I'll beckon you closer with my finger. You'll walk slowly, unsure what to expect, toward me. I'll exhale a puff from my cigar, and coming through the fog you'll find a clearer sense of self. You just don't know it yet.

I'll whisper something, and you'll have to bend down closer to hear me better above the din: "I got you."

You will look deep into my eyes and see that I'm not bullshitting you. Yep. That's the kinda fella I am.

My Line of Feeling

Look at him. Yeah, the sign language interpreter right over there.
Look at how quickly he's signing everything he hears.
Look.
Just watch.
The way the light zeroes on him.
His ears, his hands, his face: everything.
I even like the way he wears his black clothes when he works. I don't care that they don't hide his effeminacy. His hands are so clear against the black curtain of his shirt.
I envy his fingers.
The way they move like lightning, like fire. How my eyes come away with a cough of smoke. His language churns away like a train on steroids.
"I really wish I could learn sign language."
I overhear people say this all the time.
They share these little dreams with each other because the really big dreams are too hard, too frightening to contemplate. When we articulate our wish to learn how to make our hands sing, it's because we've already intuited that our voices are inadequate.
Words.
Oh, words.
It's so easy to lie. Unleash a lot of verbal diarrhea. Fill up those awkward silences between acquaintances with words that no one will ever remember.
It's only when you start listening that you record everything for playback that you start to remember.

Love is so quicksilver-elusive.

That's why I sit here in the dark. I'm a lonely man who goes to the theater now and then.

Don't bullshit me and say that I can't possibly be lonely. I mean, look at me. I'm a quadriplegic. I can't feel much of anything in my arms and legs. But here and there I can feel pockets of sensations like around my neck. That area is like a necklace. I call it my line of feeling. You caress along the blankness of me, and I will spasm in my head. It's the most erotic feeling. My brain is my cock, and my skull is my chastity belt. As humiliating it is to be washed, I live for those accidental touches along my line of feeling. I only wish their fingers would linger.

Most quads are able to talk. Me? I can't speak clearly enough to be understood by anyone, but I can blink my eyes twice for "yes" and blink once for "no." I answer questions from attendants all day long. It's like they're trying to read my mind, and most PCAs new to me don't do a good job of it. I can bob my head a bit, so that's why I have this thing in front of my chin especially when I use the computer. It's my mouse-chin. That way I can move the cursor up and down and left and right, and then a little bump for a tap. Click! The link opens up in a new browser window. Ever since this new app came out for folks with very limited movement, I'm able to communicate more. Still cumbersome, though.

After I saw the interpreter, I began watching signed videos online and got so frustrated. I almost gave up on it until I read this thing where a deaf woman said that she was very happy that American Sign Language was difficult to master. If learning to speak was difficult for her, it made perfect sense that learning ASL would be hard for hearing people.

I've tried to memorize by sight the alphabet. A. B. C. I'm sure all of us here in the audience have tried it one time or another, and don't remember much beyond the first few letters. Yes, I know how to read my name: S. T. E. V. E. Steve. See?

It's the promise of a new language, so full of secrets, that keep us sitting in the dark, watching the actors interact with each other, with an occasional glance at that interpreter standing to the side. He's all by himself.

He has a halo, an aura around his body. His hands are like wings, feathers fallen from the clouds of heaven itself. If angels existed, they wouldn't speak; they would sign. No voice could possibly compare with the mysterious silences that spark like fireflies off their hands.

That man there—well, he doesn't know I exist.

Oh, of course, here in Detroit, a lot of gay guys know each other. I'm not talking about on a first-name basis, mind you, but from the daily gallery of their faces in one hookup app too many. My attendant Rico isn't shy about showing me the guys he likes on his smartphone. He's my favorite because he knows I like to look when he's on the prowl. "What do you think?" I blink my eyes in response. Sometimes I'll woof in approval, and he always laughs. "You are wicked, man," he says. He's not ashamed of wheeling me around the city. He's so cool.

Here's the thing, though. Guys will always look for a reason to turn you down. They want you to know that you're never going to be good enough for them because they're too good for you. It's really all a show-me-how-big-you-are contest. Look at how hung I am! Look at how versatile I am! Look, look, look! That's what Rico says.

I say, Fuck all that. Since when have we become sex toys designed for the amusement of men who won't even ask for our names? Whatever happened to the rest of ourselves? How have we become that disposable?

It's as if the spotlight is permanently fixated on between our legs. We are nothing without our cocks. We're not even people.

People, stop looking down here and start looking up at our faces.

I mean, look at him!

That man.

I love the way he takes his interpreting work seriously.

He's the most beautiful soul I've seen all my life.

The way he allows anyone to meditate on him and the way he accepts your gaze without knowing who you are, without expecting you to demand comprehension. If you don't need ASL to communicate, he isn't for you.

Yeah.

He inspires me. I know it's a cliché when a disability is supposed to be inspirational. Hell, if you want to win an Oscar for acting, be an able-bodied person and pretend to be disabled! The notion of passing as disabled is somehow equated to the notion of conquering disability itself. We must stand up with our polio-ravaged legs! We must try harder to pronounce our mangled speech more clearly. We must do everything we can to make you feel less afraid of us.

The funny thing is, you've done everything to make us afraid of you.

You thrive on making sure that everyone looks just like you.

Hell, I look just like you. That's how I see myself in the mirror. I'm just me.

In my mind, I talk and walk like a hearing person, so therefore I must be ... normal!

I love the word "normal."

It's uplifting, the very heart of every story that able-bodied people write about disability.

Well.

Fuck "normal"!

Oh, if only he could look into my throbbing heart and see what I see. But you know how it is: you see something in someone, and no one sees what you see in him.

He's like that.

Everyone knows how much he's done for the queer community and all that. He's very kind, and he's definitely well-liked. People hug him when they meet him. He's clearly a great guy.

No, it's more than that. It runs much deeper than that.

You know how some people with really big smiles are? They're the ones who fill their Facebook newsfeed showing off how amazing and wonderful their lives are. They're the ones with partners and kids. They're always mugging with their friends in their selfies. Rico is a Facebook junkie, and he always shows me something every so often with a comment. This is how I know all this. Maybe they don't mean to make you feel like nothing, when you've got nothing compared to their breezy dispatches.

Oh, no.

Everyone loves him onstage.

That man.

Oh, that man.

It's so hard to tell him how much he means to me.

That's why I have all those inner conversations with myself. Up here in the theater of my brain there is no fourth wall. Darkness hugs me to its chest. It's all I've ever known. If I listen closely, I can hear the heart of loneliness beating. It gets very loud once you pick it out of the din of white noise, and you can't hear anything else.

Once you hear it, you learn to look for it in other people. You want to find another heart with the same beat as yours. Otherwise two hearts beating differently become a tough language to learn. Loneliness requires a certain kind of music in order for it to fade away into a symphony of contentment.

One must be the singer.

The other must be a guitar player.

The song is called "I Understand You."

You don't know the lyrics, but when the two of you start playing together, it feels absolutely right.

20

I know.

Because I did love someone a lifetime ago.

I was young and horny.

So was he.

We met in a bar.

I know this is a fantasy, but bear with me. It's a favorite of mine.

Hormones in a smoke-filled room. My eyes felt a bit scratchy because the smoke was so acrid and heavy, but I didn't want to leave since I'd waited all week to come to that bar and check out the hot guys.

His name was Allen.

He grew up in a small town up north. Nothing of note except for the timber they felled every summer and the maple syrup they tapped every winter.

When we saw each other across the room, there was for a brief moment a break through the fog of smoke. There he was, standing in his Red Wing boots and jeans and flannel shirt, and nursing a beer. He winked at me.

I winked back.

Such a simple thing, really.

That's all it took.

I strutted through that room and kissed him smack on the mouth. No names, no anything. That was my introduction. I'm gruff.

You know what he did?

He introduced himself right back with his tongue.

We were like glue after that moment.

We stayed in the bar until it closed.

He came to my place that night. We were too tired to fuck, but damn, when we woke up the next morning, we were at it like rabbits.

People will say that I confused lust with love when I say that I loved him.

I loved him because he was very kind to me.

He never said that I was stupid or slow-witted.

I wish to God that everyone could see the inside of me because they'd see I have a brain, an intelligence.

The fire in my eyes is always burning.

What you see of me now is what I want everyone in the world to see. I can walk and speak just like anyone; no thinking necessary for me to move around. I don't have to worry about how they'll gawk at me, the freak that I am. They wouldn't know that I'm that guy who sits out front with his PCA on the bus. My tongue sticks halfway out, and that can't be helped. It's my brain, you see. I don't have full control of the muscles in my face.

21

If I try to speak, I sound like an animal.

Doesn't matter that I can hear everyone perfectly.

It's astonishing how many people feel entitled to talk about me as if I can't hear them. But I do.

Every single word.

I'm always listening.

That's why I don't like words.

They hurt.

The fact that everyone requires words to "communicate" is full of bullshit.

I don't need words to survive.

I need someone not to require words of me in order to be loved.

I'm not a cute child that you can use in a poster to ask for donations.

I'm a fifty-two-year old adult male who's been called "retard" and "useless lump" at one time or another. I've been living in a group home since my mother died ten years ago.

I've never gone out on a single date.

I've never been inside a gay bar.

I've never chatted with anyone online. It takes forever to type a word with my chin.

I learn about what guys do all the time when I overhear things around me.

I'm always listening.

Always.

I can't move easily, but my ears pick up a lot more than you think. It's like sonar.

The one time someone touched me, it was a PCA. He didn't ask me for permission when he put his dick into my mouth.

I was fourteen.

He figured that because I couldn't talk well, he could get away with it.

I was confused when it was all over.

What was I?

An object. A sex toy.

I knew I was odd when I noticed how people looked at me differently. Once I understood the concept that I was a freak, I was never the same. I was five years old.

Some people say that I have the nicest eyes.

I think they only say that just like they tell fat girls the same thing: "My, what such a pretty face you have!"

Is it so hard for you to see inside this body of mine and see that I'm a James Bond, a Michelangelo, a Shakespeare, a Fred Astaire, a Casanova?

Look into my eyes.

Isn't that where my soul is?

I'm not a dog.

Don't you stare into my eyes as if I'm a dog and project pity onto me. Enough of that shit.

I'm more than just that thing that little kids point at and ask in a loud voice, "Mommy, why does he look like that?" right before she shushes them.

I'm too repellent.

I'm never going to be asked to perform on an amateur porn site.

I'm fifty-two years old, and no one ever stops to think that maybe I do want to go out on a date. Maybe sex would be nice, but it seems I'm asking for too much.

Somehow disability is equated with impotence.

We are not sexual beings.

We are still children trapped in adult bodies.

I'm here to tell you that, at least for me, I'm horny as fuck. I don't want your pity, but I would love to lie next to a naked man. I don't care how old he is. I just don't want him to look at me like I'm a freak. I want him to look at me the same way he sees a hot man on the street.

Yeah.

I have a dick.

Right here.

Nobody's touched it.

Well, many attendants have touched it over the years, but they all acted as if my dick was a distasteful thing. And then there was that asshole attendant who forced himself into my mouth.

When the confusion about him faded away, I realized that because he was the only one who touched me in that way, I loved him.

No one wanted to touch me in any way, not even a pat on my shoulder to say hello.

I am carrion.

I'm lumped together with the special needs adults.

I wish I could speak so clearly, at least once in my life, to tell you that I have only one special need. A man who would love me as I am. Someone who would hold my hand in public and kiss me even when my tongue is hanging out. Someone who would be proud to say that I'm his husband.

23

You see that interpreter standing over there?

He's like an angel to me.

To him I'm just another audience member who doesn't know ASL. But if you saw deep into the heart of my brain, you'd know that I'd work very hard to master ASL.

Doesn't matter if I don't know a deaf person.

I've seen how hearing people treat deaf people all the time.

I can see in their eyes the same frustration of being treated less because they can't speak clearly. Those hearing people dumb down their talk as if these deaf adults are like children who need a gentle lecture.

I hate baby talk more than anyone will ever know.

I hear this from some of my PCAs: "Would Steve like some puréed carrots?"

I feel for anyone who feels like a freak show.

Hell, I'm a freak show on wheels!

Come on, baby, gawk at me. Why not? Admission's free!

It's good for your soul. Think chicken soup.

I want you to feel uncomfortable with this image of yourself trying to pretend that you don't gawk, but you do.

You can't help but gawk because I look exactly like what you feel like inside yourself.

I am you turned inside out. Helpless as fuck.

I am a freak so you don't have to live with looking like one.

I'm here to remind you that you are a freak.

Yes. *You.*

Everyone needs to get in touch with their inner freak show.

The men who work out and preen so their muscles shine in their selfies taken in their bathroom mirrors are absolutely evil.

They are the ones who remind us that we are all less than them.

They are the ones who've decided their own hotness so that anyone less than them can't ever be considered hot, and if we find anyone else hot, we are made to feel ashamed of ourselves.

Thank God for the bear community.

They were the ones who said, Fuck beauty. Our bellies are sexy.

And now, it seems that muscle bears have co-opted the label of "bear," because they are so hot. Perfection equals beauty, right?

We need to stop treating these muscle guys like the hottest thing since sliced bread.

We need to treat them as if they're the ugliest creatures on earth. Treat them like shit. That's what they do to other people all the time, right?

24

We need to laugh at them when they trip over in the puddle of their own arrogance.

That way they can taste blood, the same blood that I taste every day.

I know what it tastes like.

Humiliation is a flavor in all its own category. There's quite nothing like it.

Please don't tsk-tsk me if you think I'm too angry.

You'd be angry too if you had no way to express it like I do. Sometimes I bang my head against the pillow and cry. I don't want to be super-tough all the time. Being wheeled out there all the time will harden anyone.

I don't like to go out that much. Too humiliating.

Isn't that obvious?

People are mean.

Would you ever come up to me and say, "Wow, what a handsome man you are"? Not in a patronizing tone of voice, but in a genuine gush of longing and lust. For *me*.

No?

When you're afraid of me, it's because you're afraid of yourself.

You're afraid to find that I'm just like you.

Big surprise!

I'm just a gay man who's sharp as a tack, but who can't get laid because—look at me!

No one ever tells me that I'm hot.

I dream of love all the time. It hurts to watch romantic movies. Sometimes it pisses me off when I see how two able-bodied lovers bicker in a movie. Don't they know how good they have it? They don't have to deal with a tongue that sticks to the side and the looks I get on the street.

I long to lie next to a guy, have him hold me right back. I want to feel the weight of his body against mine. Heart to heart.

I long to have him tell me how much he loves me, how he can't be without me. I long to hear him whisper as he traces a finger along my line of feeling, constantly torturing me in the sweetest, sexiest way possible.

I long to have him propose marriage to me. Being someone's husband ... wow. I get sappy every time I think about such a wild possibility!

He'll never know what unconditional love means until I say, "I do." I'll even spend weeks practicing those two words until I'm crystal-clear.

A good and loving man is all I want.

Please don't behave as if I don't deserve one because of the way I look on the outside.

Please don't look at my man as if he's a sick person for choosing to love me.

Do you know why I love that interpreter so?

Maybe it was a small thing to him and I'm sure he's forgotten all about it, but it was universe-shattering for me.

Three years ago I was with my housemates from the group home to see a show called *Umbrellas on Woodward Avenue*. We got there early so we wouldn't have to hold up everyone trying to go down the aisles to their seats.

The interpreter was standing by the front seats when my PCA accidentally pushed my wheelchair too quickly over the top step. I've never liked Lou, but that was the one time I was grateful for his ineptness.

The interpreter caught me and my chair. I was strapped as usual to the back of my chair, but he didn't seem to know that.

He said, "Hey. You all right?"

He looked right into my eyes.

Imagine that. Strangers never do that with me.

It was clear from his facial expression that he'd never noticed my tongue.

He looked right into my eyes. Nothing else.

I looked right back.

I tried to speak.

I know it's not possible to believe this, but can love, pure and unadulterated, exist for less than a few seconds?

Yes, it does.

Every day I think of that moment, and it's all I need to get by. He made me feel like the human being that I am.

Maybe I'll never find someone who will accept me as I am.

So when the voice in the theater said the usual bullshit about turning off your cell phones, no photography, and so on, I was mesmerized by his signing.

No words.

I had seen ASL interpreters before, but never like this.

I don't know if he's a good interpreter or not, but I couldn't stop watching him. The musical wasn't very good, but watching him filled me with a love I didn't know I possessed. It's hard to be loving when everyone treats you as if you're lesser than them, but when he looked into my eyes, out of concern for me without that look of disgust on his face, I felt equal to him.

Yeah. Look at him.

He's a god.

Maybe you don't think he has a great body. Maybe he's not your type. Maybe he's not butch enough.

I don't care.

He's still a god.

The mark of a great man lies in not whether he leads but whether he gives out to others his kindnesses, unasked for and without hesitation.

I mean, look at him.

Just watch.

Cartography

Some people think what we do in a bathhouse is a dance. Up and down the aisles each one of us, stroking ourselves through our white terry towels wrapped around our waists, walk and peer into the cracks of doors left open to invite just about anyone to join in the grunts emanating within. The music pulsates, but we are not dancing. Our hunger is on the prowl. We need a man's touch to stay alive. Names aren't necessary for sustenance.

The darkness is my security blanket. As long as no one can see the dotted geography of psoriasis on my chest and back, I remain desirable here in Man's Land. The trick is to leave the towel wrapped around my neck and distract them with my naked goods. They never question why I wear a t-shirt when everyone else walks around shirtless.

Once a man with a peculiar accent—perhaps he was indeed from France—tried to pull up my shirt while we made out in his room. We had ejaculated a few minutes before but he wanted a second round. A red lightbulb hung over us while a Madonna remix throbbed over our heads. He was a slender man with the thickest mustache I had ever seen. I grabbed his hands and held them away from my body.

"What is so wrong?" he asked when he stopped kissing me.

"You can't touch me like that."

"Why? You have a lovely body."

"Just—just don't, okay?"

We resumed kissing.

His hands suddenly grabbed the front of my shirt and pulled it up. His eyes widened. "*Shite!*"

He grabbed his towel and left the room. He never gave me a chance to explain that psoriasis wasn't contagious.

I didn't go back for a month. Nightmares of everyone finding out about my scaly splotches plagued me. My dermatologist said that the topical treatment I was taking was the strongest for my particular condition. "It'll probably never completely go away," he said, "but the flaking should be vastly reduced."

Each time I lather the ointment on my body is an act of prayer.

I am always grateful that people are required to wear clothes. I always wear a white undershirt under my long-sleeved shirt at the office. I look like a dork, but at least I appear to be like everyone else. No one has to know what's underneath my layers.

This is why I like living up north even though I don't care for snow. A longer winter means that I can continue to hide even in the sunlight.

When I returned, a few regulars whose names I have never known suddenly asked me, "Where you been?" I was surprised that they'd noticed.

"Sick," I said. "I was out sick."

"Well, glad to see you're doin' okay."

I didn't connect with anyone that night. I didn't feel so free to wander like before. Someone had charted the atlas of my fear.

The steam, thick and langorous, rises and shields only the faces of those who've splayed their legs apart on a towel. Something inevitably happens. This is why the steam room is so popular.

When I went in there once, I didn't take off my t-shirt and sat down. No one made a move toward me. I closed my eyes and took deep breaths.

My bones sighed with pleasure.

Time slowed down. A minute felt like an hour. The steam was drawing every ounce of tension from my body.

I fell into a blissful trance, and then my lungs felt tight. I had to leave.

When I stood out in the slight chilly hallway, I found my shirt plastered to my chest. I was not surprised by this, but I could see my dark bumps through the white fabric. I didn't have a spare in my locker.

I went into a bathroom stall, sat down on the toilet, and wrung my shirt again and again until there was no water left to milk. I walked home with my wet shirt on underneath my jacket. I was afraid of catching pneumonia, but I didn't care.

I dream often of falling backward into a vast puddle of powder that resembles cocaine. As the white puffs outward in my wake, I rock and roll from side to side until I feel the tiny incisor teeth of the invisible white monsters scratching my back like a coin against a lottery ticket until the splotches are gone. I would be forever reborn from the kiss of dawn with a skin so translucent that every man would beg to lick all over my sweating body.

The darkness in Man's Land masks the signs of aging on my face. I have seen the young men working downstairs come and go. I don't remember all of their names, but I'm sure they all remember me as that t-shirt guy. I've lost track of the years traveling in this place.

I am grateful that none of the regulars ever questions me why.

Who knew that such a thin fabric could be of armor quality?

Just another evening: I nod hello at the regulars whispering in conversation. I walk, seeking out potential prey. The few guys all look away when they catch my interest. It is a slow night, but I'm not worried. I move back to the locker room where I await the deluge of guys to come.

Like clockwork, they do. Something innate inside us men tells us to congregate at specific times, unbidden, and this is why it pays to wait. Some of them are so horny they don't ask about my shirt. They just want to get off, and right now. I pleasure three guys, one after another.

But it is not enough. I am still ugly.

Nights when I'm not at Man's Land I watch TV. The canned laughter and babble do not fill the emptiness in my soul. I like my job and my co-workers, but all they talk about are spouses and kids. They know I'm gay, but they never ask if I have a boyfriend. I'm just that guy who researches and prints out highly-detailed maps for road construction guys who need to know precisely where the buried power lines and water pipes are.

Am I truly that unattractive?

Tonight I find myself too restless to watch TV.

I check the weather outside. Not rainy at all.

I shower and choose a fresh t-shirt.

I am inside Man's Land before I know it. The place is familiar as any map I've studied. I know which doors have loose hinges, where the cracks in the floor are, and what the true hues of red and purple in the paint are. Sometimes if I catch an attendant mopping the floor with a bucket of disinfectant, I point out what needs to be fixed.

So up and down the aisles I go.

Familiar faces, all. Some I've played with before glance at me. They want an encore. I whisper, "Not tonight."

I want somebody so new that I can forget my shirt for a moment.

It is not long before I see him in the locker room. He takes off his khakis. He looks like a computer programmer.

He is a foot shorter than me. A little stocky, but nothing to be ashamed of. He appears to be twenty years younger than me. He looks cute with his stubble. One might say that, in the bear community's parlance, he is a cub. But he doesn't take off his loose V-neck shirt.

He knows I am watching, but his face reveals nothing. As he wraps himself in a towel, he takes in my shirt. He leaves for the aisles.

I follow him up and down the aisles. His halting pace makes it clear that he hasn't been here before.

I wait when he peers into the steam room.

He makes his rounds a second time.

I pace myself without seeming desperate. This is a familiar game.

He finally stops. He turns and looks at me. The question in his discerning eyes is hard to read.

I say nothing. I am a shadow.

He comes closer and whispers. "Psoriasis?"

My eyes fill with panic.

He grabs my hand and pulls me into the nearest available room. There, under the red bulb, he says, "Hey. Me, too."

He pulls up his shirt. His chest looks worse than mine. His self-confidence takes my breath away. In his moment of fearlessness I find him the hottest man alive.

I inhale and peel off my shirt. I am afraid to look directly at his face.

He smiles.

Surprised, I give a short laugh of relief.

As I allow his hands to roam lightly all over the virgin islands of my chest, I am shocked to see in his eyes the beautiful atlas that is my body. He wipes away my quiet tears and says, "Hey, man. I know."

This time I will not stay a stranger. I will learn his name and give him mine. Together we will draw a new cartography.

September Song

You've always liked riding with Mom on the train from Long Island to Manhattan, and walking around with her on Fifth Avenue, because there are so many things to see. Men in hats and suits and shiny shoes always step aside for you and Mom when she holds your hand. Women in hats and dresses and heels also holding hands of their children nod acknowledgment to Mom and you as they pass. The din of their feet and conversations as they pass by is punctuated by the exclamations of a megaphone exhorting that everyone buy war bonds to help support the U.S. effort, and the occasional cry of a man holding up a newspaper and shouting the latest headlines about the fight against Hitler. Amidst the flurry of pedestrians you spot a skinny woman with curly hair swinging her legs in braces and wooden crutches forward as her brown purse bangs in rhythm. The hosiery on one of her legs has a tear that runs from her knee down to her foot. Her face is lined with a map of wrinkles made from far too many gawks. When she sees you, you wave a small hello. She lights up with a smile at you before the pedestrians swell up around her. She disappears.

You follow Mom down Fifth Avenue. As you two pass St. Thomas Church, you spot a legless young man wearing an old sweater and sitting on a shallow box with wheels. Before him is an upturned cap littered with coins and a sign that says PLEASE HELP — GOD BLESS. His eyes are almost the same height as yours, and you stop in spite of yourself. How could a person be without legs? Mom pulls you away sharply and says, "Don't gawk."

All that day you think about that man. You wonder what it's like not to have legs. Your dreams in the shadow of moonlight from then on were filled with endless whispers. You cannot see their faces, but you know they are freaks. They'd have to be, because why else would they hide? You look at yourself in the mirror and see again how perfectly made you are: regular height and weight, full use of arms and legs, and a face that older women feel compelled to pinch while exclaiming what a cute little boy you are.

Because you were born two weeks after Hitler invaded Poland, you have grown up overhearing about the war, but nothing has punctured the bubble of your dreaming. Dad could not serve in the war because he received a 4-F for having flat feet. Many of your friends have fathers and uncles serving in the war overseas in Europe and the Pacific. The names of these places do not have any meaning to you; the atlas that your mother shows you reveal one squiggly drawing with clusters of names after another. You cannot fathom the distance from your house on Sweetbriar Street to the bloody attack launched on the Normandy Beach, especially after when Mom explains that getting to Europe is like a hundred times longer than the train ride to Manhattan and back. You like the way President FDR smiles so gregariously even with a cigarette holder in his mouth, the bushiness of his eyebrows, and the large size of his hands as he waves. You never learn until years later how polio, which attacked him when he was 39 years old, had prevented him from walking, and how he took great pains never to be photographed in a wheelchair.

In time you stop dreaming about freaks. They have been swept away like dust underneath the bed. You are too busy hopping on your Schwinn bike and chasing your neighborhood buddies. There is always another adventure to be had, another prank to execute, a round of gut-clutching guffaws.

Then for a startling moment, amidst the euphoria of the war ending, you spot something different about the returning soldiers here and there when you join your parents for the big victory parade in downtown Manhattan. They have missing forearms. They roll by in wheelchairs. They hobble along with crutches. Their faces have deep scars from shrapnel. Some sport eye patches. And a few have in their eyes a permanent look of being forever lost. They are the ones who speak the language of fear the loudest. You wonder just what they've seen.

When you are seven years old, your parents take you to Coney Island one hot August evening. The sprawl of bright yellows and pinks and blues spuming from the west matches the colors of cotton candy spun around a white paper stick. The sugar explodes on your tongue as the moon bobs on the ocean waves. Mom smiles happily at you. Dad has been busy lately with his job; he has been traveling a good deal now that he is an executive at a Madison Avenue advertising agency. You rarely see him these days, but Mom talks a great deal about what a good man he is to go great lengths to provide for his family. You don't notice how soft and husky her voice becomes after a few drinks. She tells you to go to bed earlier and earlier until you try to sleep with the last wisps of sun leaking into your window.

But now that your parents are together, everything is all right again. Lights, strung from one hook to another, cast a spell of color and shadow among the scruffy grass blades that seek sanctuary from people tromping past. Music calliope from rickety speakers perched atop posts. Laughs and squeals amplify and recede into the dark as teenagers spin and coast on rides past you and your parents. A barrel-chested barker with the ends of his mustache waxed into hooks calls out to Dad, daring him to try his hand at shooting down one of the metal ducks spinning around. "Get a prize for your boy," he cajoles.

Dad relents. He doesn't succeed after twelve tries.

The barker winks at you and plucks a stuffed orange tiger from the wall above the ducks. "Hey, kid. Want this little tiger?"

You nod, and catch. You hold it up to your parents. "Look what I got!"

They beam.

As you cradle the tiger, you feel warm. You have a new friend. You will name him LTR, as in Little Tiger Roosevelt.

All evening you walk around with your parents and absorb the smell of caramel popcorn and the sizzle of hot dogs. Young couples hold each other's hands as they point out a sight past Dad and talk into each other's ears amidst the din.

A shadow flickers across Dad's face as Mom suddenly pulls him closer. Her laughter is clear and hard as lacquer.

You would remember this night as the last time you saw them happy together.

Days later you overhear their voices, shrill and accusing and defensive. Nora is a name you hear a lot. Dad comes home less and less until you wonder if you are seeing a ghost whenever he walks up to the front door and takes you out to a park, a museum, a zoo. He never asks you questions about how Mom is doing. You never tell him how she passes out enough times that you've set up your alarm clock to wake you up at midnight to bring down a blanket to the living room and cover her on the sofa so she wouldn't be cold. You also don't tell him about the looks you've gotten from some of your classmates because your parents have divorced. You don't tell him how lonely you've become. You are just happy to see Dad again. He rarely talks about Nora or even living in the city. He is all smiles and a haze of cigarette smoke when he drives you back to your house.

You dread the moment when you enter the house and find Mom ready to machine-gun you with questions about your father. Did he say anything about Nora? Or having kids? Or buying a place on the Upper East Side? Or maybe near Gramercy Park?

Your answer is always the same: "He never tells me anything."

In time Mom gives up all pretense of not drinking. She doesn't fix up her hair anymore; she spends entire days in a bathrobe in front of the scratchy-voiced television set. She orders everything to be delivered to the house: groceries, cigarettes, and liquor. She doesn't notice how much you've changed until she hears a lower register in your voice. "Hey. You okay?"

"Yeah," you mumble.

By then you've fallen in with a crowd of troublemakers. Many of them come from broken homes, so they wear their defiance like tattoos on their biceps in the hallways and outside the side doors to the school. They smoke cigarettes, talk big tits, and grease their hair. You play along, but you are the quiet one in the group. You have no words to describe the feelings that overcome your body each time you see Sonny Pears. You identify intensely with Sal Mineo, the actor who played a character smitten with James Dean's character in *Rebel Without a Cause*. You've seen the film at the theater seven times.

Growing up, you had never paid much attention to Sonny. He was the first in his class to have divorced parents. For years he was the only fat boy in class. He never seemed to care whether the tails of his shirt were tucked into his pants, or whether his shoes were tied. At times it seemed as if he'd never bathed. You saw how your teacher tried not to flinch when she talked to him.

When your parents told you that they were divorcing, you didn't know what to think. You had seen how Sonny, and then Cathy and Joey, were treated at school. They were outcasts. You didn't want to join them. You burst into tears and ran upstairs to your room. Somehow or the other you fell into a deep sleep, and you woke up to find Mom sitting in your room. She didn't look drunk, but the angel of emotion had left her body. She was a statue waiting for you to wake up so she could make herself the first coffee, the first drink of the day. You froze when you saw her sitting still. Had you done something wrong? It wasn't like Mom to be like this. The softness, the easy chuckles, the fluid gait—all gone. Her presence was there, but she was not there. The mother you loved was gone, and she left you a shell of memories. She eventually gave up on making sandwiches for your lunchbox and cooking dinners. "You can eat cornflakes if you want," she said.

When you came back to school after that summer, Sonny wasn't fat anymore. He had become sleek like a cat. He rolled up the sleeves of his t-shirt to reveal his lean biceps and the hems of his dungarees to show off his Chuck Taylors. He had taken to smoking. He drove a souped-up hotrodder that clacked occasionally when he shifted gears. When he invited you to join his gang, you tried to be casual. "Sure."

You learn how to smoke, laugh at dirty jokes, perfect your brooding, and jack off to the fantasy of Sonny kissing you full-throttle on the mouth like the way he did to Brenda Witt. When he brags about how she went down on him, you long to be her, the school tramp who'd do anything for a touchy-feely, the tongue and the mouth consuming him whole down to the root. Instead you hold a lit match to a fresh cigarette and inhale deeply as he brags about his finger exploring her pussy.

You join Sonny and the boys in his jalopy on a spur-of-the-moment trip to the city, but Sonny makes a wrong turn on the expressway. You spot a billboard pointing that way to Coney Island and shout, "Look! Why don't we go there?"

"Yeah! Let's!" the boys chorus.

Sonny gives you a wink. You wonder if his left turn was accidental after all.

At Coney Island the five of you walk up and down the boardwalk. They turn quiet after seeing so many pretty girls clad in only swimsuits. You stay quiet when you see the wide variety of men of all ages and sizes, all shirtless, walking around in swim trunks. They seem to be from another world. You are surprised when a few catch your gaze and smile back. You look about yourself. Did he really look at you?

Then Sonny says, "Let's go to the freak show."

Off to the side is a burlap-heavy tent through which the five of you laugh helplessly at the contortions of their facial expressions at a funhouse mirror. The other boys move on to the next mirror, but Sonny remains standing next to you. He leans his head forward a little, and you lean back just so. His forehead turns elongated as the bottom half of his face shrivels into a sharp goatee. Your cheekbones swell as you smile. You turn to Sonny, and just as he's about to turn to you, you catch his startled look when you appear to be kissing his cheek—no, his lips!—as he turns to you. He jumps back.

You are about to apologize, but you stop. Why apologize if it was only visual trickery, right?

Sonny doesn't look at you.

You follow him with the boys, already waiting in line. Around you are garish paintings that promise unforgettable sights of souls trapped in their physical wretchedness. A long-haired woman with a nose earring gussied up in gypsy clothes and steps out to accept your ticket with her faux jewel-laden fingers. You follow the gang to the second row of folding chairs. A tinny speaker plays music that sounds like voodoo. You glance around the makeshift theater. The heavy canvas walls have been painted a dark blue. The mauve curtains have a few patches of almost the right shade sewn on. More people fill the seats. The theater seems to turn hotter.

An overweight man, wearing a top hat and a jacket painted to look as if snakes are writhing all over his body, adjusts his red cummerbund before he picks up the microphone. "Ladies and gentlemen! Thank you for coming in here on a fine summer day. You've seen the beauties on the boardwalk, so it's time to see the beasts. When you see them for the first time, don't scream. They might jump off this very stage and attack you! Don't worry, though. We got folks back here who know how to tame them. But first, a bit of New York history."

In his mellifluous voice, he shares a story about a beautiful couple who lived a long time ago at the Five Points neighborhood in lower Manhattan. *Nearby was a pond known as Collect Pond, and everyone drank from it. The problem was, people dumped the contents of their chamberpots into the pond.* The audience lets loose a long "Euuuuuwww!" *One day Jill Knickerbocker, the wife of a wealthy sea merchant and a descendant of the peg-legged Peter Stuyvesant, took ill not long after she turned pregnant. She had to stay in bed, and when she slept, she had disturbing dreams about Collect Pond. It was harboring a most horrible serpent that came out only to devour freshly born babies. But her husband Jack Knickerbocker, after having heard these dreams described in great detail, knew what to do. He had a lot of experience with hunting whales. He brought together a group of friends and came up with a plan. When his wife started to feel the pains of her oncoming birth, two men would stand guard at the door to her bedroom while the two midwives assisted with the delivery. He and the other men would stand guard with their spears and harpoons ready in front of their house on Center Street. Finally the long-awaited day arrived, so the guards and midwives took their places. As Mrs. Knickerbocker moaned and wailed from the pains embroiled inside her womb, Collect Pond began to churn. Everyone in the neighborhood fled the area. Five Points was empty for the first time since the Dutch arrived in Manhattan and took it from the Indians.*

Mr. Knickerbocker and his men turned steely-eyed as they caught reflections of sun shimmering from the scales covering the body of a large serpent as it sloshed among the lily pads. Then it sailed right out of the water and slithered like a bird across the sky and right over the rowhouses. It had a huge head with a pair of yellow eyes and a dark purple forked tongue that flicked out of hunger. Its stench was worse than twenty outhouses combined. As the great monster swooped down toward the front door of the Knickerbocker residence, the men positioned themselves and flung their harpoons.

But the sharp tips could not puncture the slimy scales. The serpent opened its mouth and snapped up the men like they were lunch. Mr. Knickerbocker barely escaped and ran off to the side. Meanwhile his wife was in the final throes of giving birth. The monster belly-slimed up the stairs. It chewed up the guards and managed to slip halfway through the bedroom door. There in the hands of the midwives was a beautiful baby boy. Mrs. Knickerbocker saw the monster and fainted dead away. The midwives turned their bodies away from the monster and huddled together to protect the baby, but it was no good. A tiny drop of saliva from the monster's lips fell on the baby's forehead. The baby cried and writhed as he grew a serpent's tail. The midwives were horrified by the sight of the monsterious baby.

At that very moment Mr. Knickerbocker had climbed up the battered stairs with a few harpoons in hand. He noticed how the serpent opened its scales like tiny mouths. He punctured the pink flesh underneath the scales in the tail and jumped over the railing just as the tail thrashed about from the pain. The monster couldn't move very well now that it was stuck in the doorway. Mr. Knickerbocker climbed atop the monster and slipped through the upper half of the doorway. Just as the monster twisted and turned its head, Mr. Knickerbocker lifted his last two spears in both hands and stabbed the monster's eyes at the same time. The monster convulsed so much that it knocked the midwives and the furniture. The serpent-baby flew up through the air right into his father's arms.

Then the baby opened its mouth. It had sharp little teeth.

There was no greater sorrow in the world than having to kill your own child in order to save New York City. Yes, Mr. Knickerbocker had to strangle his firstborn. The Knickerbockers went mad and became destitute, and the city filled up Collect Pond with rocks and paved new streets over it so there would be no more serpents.

The emcee turns to the audience. "But we still have one more monster." He points to a box set on a tiny table. Somehow in the middle of his rapturous storytelling you have never noticed the table being brought onstage. He pulls out a handkerchief from his jacket and drops it into the box. He lifts what appears to be a jar and brings it to the front lip of the stage. He pulls the handkerchief away to reveal a jar filled with resin-colored formaldehyde and a fetus with a thick snake tail twisted around its body. "Monsters still live among us!"

The audience screams as the lights suddenly black out.

You are stunned.

Lights soon return and fill the stage. The emcee smiles with a chuckle. "Ladies and gentlemen, please welcome to the best freak show in the world!"

The freaks of nature soon parade by on the stage. The audience gasps after each introduction. You overhear the occasional cry of "I think I'm gonna throw up" among the audience, but the sounds of vomiting do not come. There's always another freak coming onstage.

You see a diminutive-sized couple dance a minuet with each other. They are dressed as if they come from Mozart's time in Vienna. The background set is a ballroom set in miniature, replete with embroidered chairs and drapes; everything has been resized to their proportions.

A bearded lady prances slowly around the stage to a burlesque version of Peggy Lee's "Fever." She is wearing a silk dress that not only reveals her curves but also the valley of her cleavage, and her black beard seems real. Her eyebrows are thick as night. As she does a charade of burlesque without ever removing a single item of clothing, her eyes strike you as made of glass. Yes, she could clearly see everything around her and moves around without tripping, but she is an empty shell. She has no soul left. You unexpectedly recall Mom, and you try not to cry.

But the last one hits you hard. Ted and Ned Darling, a conjoined twin in their forties, appear in tuxedos with arms around each other as a Duke Ellington record plays. They are joined through the stomach. Their four legs move and tap-dance as one. Your jaw drops at their insect-like dexterity. You turn to Sonny and catch a look of revulsion on his face.

You look back to the stage, and the Darlings have caught you looking at Sonny. They do not smile at you, but as the song winds down to a loud applause, they give Sonny a look of angry defiance. If their eyes could burn anyone to death, Sonny would've been ashes in an instant.

Sonny averts his eyes. "Let's get the fuck outta here," he mumbles. He doesn't wait for the emcee to return to the stage and thank the audience.

Afterward on the boardwalk the sun shimmering from the ocean hurts your eyes. The five of you do not say anything for a few minutes.

"Fucking freaks," Sonny says at last. "Fucking dumb show."

As the boys revel in their adrenaline of discovery and revelation, you stay quiet. Later, when you are finally alone in your bedroom, you try to fall asleep. You can't. You can't stop thinking of the Darlings: their eyes so full of embittered rage. You wonder what it'd be like to be forever enjoined to Sonny, your arms around him as always with his face so close to yours.

Everyone in Sonny's gang but you eventually gets arrested for stealing and vandalizing. You are grateful that you have to look after Mom so you can't always run with them late at night. The house has become silent like a funeral parlor. What's missing are a few potted lilies, a coffin, and Mom's body in it.

Now crag-faced with a creeping belly, Dad demands to know why you've become sullen and monosyllabic. He enters your house for the first time in years and spots Mom, long gone to seed, bra-less in her bathrobe and giggling in her stupor. A few empties are strewn by the sofa.

Within days the court orders you to move in with Dad, and you are to start at a new school near his apartment in Yorkville, a posh neighborhood in Manhattan. Dad doesn't allow you to have a chance to say good-bye to Sonny and the gang. You don't like your new school at all, but you grudgingly wear a shirt and tie and slacks. You look at your classmates who carry about an air of entitlement, and you long for Sonny. No matter how heavily he'd smoked, he was always a breath of fresh air. You make a few friends, but there is nothing like the banter and the closeness of your gang.

You are surprised by how well you get along with your new stepmother. Nora works full-time as a secretary at the agency where Dad works, and she is the first woman to treat you like an adult. She never tells you how to dress or behave or clean up your room. Dad still travels a great deal, but Nora doesn't fret over his absences. One afternoon you accidentally catch her kissing a stranger in a business suit in the foyer just before he leaves the apartment.

Nora turns and sees your look of shock. She sits on the sofa and pats the empty space next to her. You oblige. She says, "If you want, you can tell your father about what's happened. He won't be upset."

"Why?"

"Because we have what's called an open marriage. He sleeps with other women, and I sleep with other men. This happens only when he's out of town." She looks at you. "One day you'll understand. It's just that we've both been in marriages where someone was always cheating. Isn't it better to be honest, and let and let live?"

You don't know what to say.

You wonder if you'll ever marry. A few girls have given you a lingering look, but you feel shy and unsure about what to do. How does a guy ask a girl out? But more than that, you feel safer in jacking off to some memory of a young handsome man you spotted on the street earlier in the day.

Mom eventually recovers after two years in a sanitarium. Purged of drink, she seems like an old woman in simply-cut clothes that seem like armor. When she talks about wanting you back home like the way things used to be, you realize how much of a shock she will be in once she learns that her house was sold to help pay off her massive debts. You say nothing. Let Dad's attorney break the news.

By then you've graduated from high school. You have no college plans. Not even trade school.

That summer you return to the town where you grew up and look for Sonny. You ask around the pool halls where you used to frequent with Sonny's gang, and you learn he's signed up for the Army. You can't imagine him taking orders from a sergeant.

You end up traveling with a company that rents out amusement rides to the county fairs around New York State with a few weekends in New Jersey. You are among the many guys who drive the rides on flatbed trucks and work seamlessly together to assemble each ride and hook up the electrical cables and test them. It's mindless work with long hours, but you feel comfortable among the guys. They remind you of your old gang, except that they wear the pockmarked patina of age. Their language is saltier than any you've heard, and many of them have served in World War II.

You end up in charge of the Ferris wheel, which everyone calls Rosie. You know every little thing that needs to be known about her and her moods. You have disassembled and reassembled Rosie so many times that you swear you could do the entire wheel in your sleep. You stand guard at the gate and press the shift button once you're satisfied that the couple is safely locked in before the wheel swings upward.

Then you watch their looks of amazement and glee as Rosie spins slowly round and round, until their ten minutes are up. It takes sixteen minutes to swing down each seat, help each couple off, and point to the next couple to step right up for their turn. You don't mind the work at all. There is always something new to see when the husbands and boyfriends stand next to their women. Some of them are handsome in an unconventional way—a permanent cut on the lip or a bulbous nose or thick bushy eyebrows—but you like that. They remind you of Sonny.

42

After you visit Dad and Nora, you decide to walk the entire way from Yorkville to Grand Central. You realize you need to piss so you stroll right into Lord & Taylor's, an upscale department store. You ask for directions to the men's room, so you take the elevator to the third floor. As you relieve yourself at a urinal, you overhear whispers between two men who seem to be hiding in the stall farthest away from you.

"—don't do Saks or Tiffany's. Too dangerous—"

"But where else can I go?"

"The Village. That's where all the queers live."

At that moment, someone opens the door to the restroom, and the conversation stops.

You don't venture out to Greenwich Village, but when you are on the road, you linger in dank restrooms and decode the language of glances and gropes. It is not long before you join the clique of men driven by desires no one can risk naming out loud. You cannot get enough of their furtive camaraderie. Even though you engage in oral sex, you don't see yourself as a cocksucker. You just have needs, that's all. Just like everyone else you know. Their cries of orgasm stifled by the fear of being caught echoes in your dreams when you are on your bunk. You are rarely alone in your trailer; three other men share it too. No one needs to know.

It is now September, and you are 25 years old. All summer you have heard nothing but the Beatles on the radio, and you are sick and tired of them. The nip of chill is already in the air, but you have one more weekend with Rosie. She has held up well all summer, and you are proud of how smoothly she runs. A group of guys have asked you to join them to go south to Florida where you can help clean up after the animals for a circus wintering there. All afternoon the skies stay overcast with a threat of rain, so business is slow.

At last the lights are turned on. The midway, once muted, flares up with laughs. The rides begin to spin and sing with screams. The smells from the concession stands waft along on the wind. You are relieved to hear the Beach Boys singing on the speakers. Anything but the goddamn Beatles.

The darkness enveloping the fair makes it easy for everyone to forget the rain supposedly to come, and you are all smiles as you beckon one couple after another aboard. Rosie will shine tonight, and you will extend her usual ride by three minutes. You have waited all day for business, so you want to treat these people extra-special.

One by one the couples are seated, and one empty car is left. You turn and spot a gruff-faced man in a wheelchair holding up a ticket for the ride. His eyes are the color of sapphire. He sports a scrawny stubble and a tank top, and the bottom half of his jeans are folded and safety-pinned underneath his knees.

"You want to get on, sir?" you ask.

He glances at the swinging car and then at you. His eyes pierce you like a dart. Your usual demeanor of a simple smile vanishes. He sees you. He has seen you. He knows what you are. He has seen you somewhere before, but he is thinking long and hard about just where. Once he figures that out, he'll proclaim to everyone that you're a cocksucker, a faggot, a queer, that you'd kneel down before any man, that you'd degrade yourself to the whims of strangers in rest rooms where the smell of piss and shit persist in spite of the ammonia-laden disinfectant mopped away. "I'm not a lightweight pillow," he says. "If you can find another fella to lift me up, well, that would help."

"Hold on."

You glance around and spot Larry two rides over. His Hurricane has no riders. You wave him over. You have always liked his easy laugh. He is tall and sturdy with a beer belly. When he comes through the gate, he sizes up the situation instantly and navigates the wheelchair closer to the empty car.

You and Larry lean forward, and the man in the wheelchair places his arms around your and Larry's necks. As you and Larry slide hands underneath the man, you catch a whiff of the man's essence. You inhale all at once his Marlboros and beer and hot dog and mustard and onion and sweat. You have the strangest urge to pull him closer to you and kiss him right on the mouth. You have never kissed a man. It is simply not done. You want to squeeze the ampleness of his ass, but you don't.

You and Larry trade glances back at the car, which is slightly swinging, and time your movements perfectly so the man is brought onto the seat without its edge banging against him.

You clang the front bar shut and clack its lock. "Have a good ride."

"Thanks," he says. His broad smile ignites a little fire inside you.

You watch him as Rosie spins gracefully. He nods at you when he swings down past you and Larry. His wheelchair is next to you.

You nod back without smiling. You don't want to give yourself away.

As Rosie swings, you check your watch. It is soon time to slow down the ride and stop. You know her so well that you're able to time it so that the man is the last to get off. For once you are happy there isn't anyone waiting in line.

You and Larry haul the man from the seat to his wheelchair. You feel a rush of adrenaline when you sense the weight of his arm wrapped around your shoulder.

"Thanks," the man says when he pushes himself back into his chair.

"Anytime," Larry says. "See ya." He returns to the Hurricane.

The man looks up at you. "Thank you."

"You're welcome. Umm, what's your name?"

"Al."

"Mick here."

You shake hands with him. He is all warmth. You don't want to let him go.

He studies you for a moment, but you don't know what the fuck for.

"What?"

"You're a homo."

"What? What are you talking about?"

"You know what I'm talking about."

"No, I don't," you say automatically.

He glances around and smiles at you. "It's okay if you are. Fellas like you were always nice to me after I got my legs chopped off, so I don't care if you're that way. Doesn't matter none to me."

"I'm sorry, I don't—"

"Look at me. *You* looked at me. Everybody pretends I'm not there, and if they see me, all they want to do is to thank me for serving in Germany. Or they act like I'm a freak show. Dames think that if you got your legs chopped off, you got your dick chopped off too. Damn, I can't find me a girl. But you—you're different. You didn't get flustered or tell me that I can't go up alone or it's unsafe for me to get on the ride. That's all I want from anyone."

You try to find your voice. "You're welcome."

He looks up at you. "Well, I should get going."

"Okay."

"You're a good man. Remember that."

That night you cannot fall asleep. You swear you will never haunt the rest rooms again. Too dangerous anyways. You will quit Rosie once you've disassembled her for the last time and find something steady year-round in Manhattan where you settle down in an efficiency studio. Maybe you could live in the Village. There has to be a place, maybe a bar, where men like you congregate discreetly and trade more than just glances. You are tired of never connecting with anyone. This time you will wrap your arms, your entire body, around him late at night. You won't care if he is an amputee. All you want—*right now*, as you grip the throbbing ache between your legs—is to sit alone with him in a car atop Rosie and weave your fingers into his secretly as the two of you look down on the vast glittery world lit by his eyes.

This

Dwight was onstage, dancing. His long limbs were sturdy like old oaks yet lithe enough to skip and hop like a tumbleweed. I wanted each bead of his sweat. I felt the music of his shadow body louder than the volume tremoring through my seat. I couldn't help but grind against the emptiness of my chair while I watched. I sensed certain men and women, especially the whites, in the audience were feeling the same way as I. There is nothing like seeing someone you love for the first time. Nothing.

For over ten years, people knew Dwight and I were friends. Some people said that we were lovers. Everyone agreed on two things though: that dancing together we matched perfectly, and that Dwight was absolutely unforgettable. But he was always a lit match in danger of going out before its time. I tried to stop him but—sometimes, even though I know better, I wonder if he even actually existed.

Every time I try to remember him, he always changes. Like mercury.

Dwight wore a pseudo-Josephine Baker banana outfit that night: the way those fake bananas flopped only reminded me of what needed to be released. Even though I always felt attracted to men more masculine than him, I was smitten.

I was nineteen at the time.

I know. Oh, how I know.

When I saw him again, prancing about in the hallway before a dress rehearsal with his dance class, I was already lost in the jungle of his eyes. Something so forceful about him scared me. Nothing in all my years of being mainstreamed in hearing schools around Chicago prepared me for this force of nature. Even though I was black, it seemed I was never black, white, hearing, or straight enough.

I used my best speech: "Hello. You danced so wonderfully."

He continued pulling at his stockings.

I waved for his attention.

He looked up. "What?"

Again, I tried to speak: "Couldn't you hear me?"

His jaw dropped when he noticed my hearing aids. I had something of an Afro at the time.

"Oh, my God. I thought everyone knew about me. The 'deaf' Dwight." He gestured and pointed to his ears. "I lost my hearing when I was fifteen."

I was more stupefied than he was: I'd found another black deaf dancer like me. I gestured and spoke: "But you do dance so well."

He smiled. "Let's see you dance."

"What? You want to see me dance? Oh, no. I'm a nobody. I couldn't."

"I'll show you more of mine if you show me yours." He gave me a wink that made it clear he was gay.

How could anyone resist?

In the rehearsal room I tried to ignore the curious glances of dancers working out. They stopped when Dwight clapped his hands and directed me to start from one corner. "You don't need music. The music has to come from within you. When I lost my hearing, that's what I had to learn."

"Well, okay. Okay. You have to remember, I didn't expect to dance today."

I had absolutely no idea of what I was doing with my body, but all I felt was the reckless soaring off into space, the heart pumping in all my veins, the madness of letting go until I crashed onto the floor. Whoops.

I looked up: the dancers were laughing hysterically.

All except one.

Dwight lifted me up and gave them the evil eye. "He can't hear worth a shit, but he's got more rhythm than any of you—combined."

With that, Dwight took my elbow and my old life out the door.

Dwight could still speak and lipread me pretty well; but he didn't like sign language too much. It made his deafness too obvious in a person already obvious in the first place. Perhaps because he couldn't hear, he never felt the eyes staring and jaws dropping whenever he boarded the El in one of his outrageous outfits. I'll never forget the looks he got when he wore a fuchsia ballet tutu. I mean, this was *1979* in Chicago!

I'll never forget what he said to me in the hallway after my first public embarrassment: "Aghhhh! You were wonderful, wonderful, wonderful! I never thought I'd get to meet anyone who could dance as good as me. Aghhh! I'm so grateful, and so honored you'd dance a little. Oh, oh. What's your name again, my dear?" He posed like a woman proud of her bikini body, and it was the first time I found such poses incredibly sexy.

"Curt. Curt Higgs."

"Curt? Oh, that's such a lovely name. Some of my best boyfriends's names began with an 'A,' as in 'apple,' but their last names also began with an 'A,' as in 'asshole.' Aghh! Oh, oh. Look at me, darling. Do you think you and I could get away and form a *real* dance company of our own? Oh, oh, come on now. Why must you be so afraid, darling? It isn't healthy."

He was everything that my father had warned me against.

Dad thought dancing was the most sissified thing to do. Male professional dancers weren't meant to exist, period. The first time I put on stage makeup for my first public performance, I pretended to speak to him, wishing more than ever that he knew signs: "Dad? Guess what? I'm putting on makeup like when I was five years old, standing on top of the toilet and trying to look at my own face with Mommy's makeup smeared and smudged all over my face. I wanted to be as beautiful as she was, not the shadow of a son I was in your eyes. Because you hated the way I turned out, you pushed my brother Harry to go out for football. Football? Like—who cares for football? I remember you sitting there in your favorite chair and watching TV and slapping your thighs when the Green Bay Packers edged over the Minnesota Vikings. I had to wonder whether you also liked to watch the jockstraps cutting corners of the players' moon asses. I was a shadow in your eyes. I was too sissy, too short, and too shy to get anywhere up the skyscrapers in your eyes. You were always looking into the fierce eyes of the sun, praying for the rays to fall upon Harry's vision and make him golden in ways I couldn't be. I was your pure gloom, your pure shame, your pure humiliation."

But the stage: there, the unquantifiable could become the quantifiable:

star. A star! I knew I could shine like the brightest star on Broadway. The Great White Way burbled up in my soul even though I hadn't the slightest idea of how to reach that.

Mom worked days, sometimes nights, at the hospital three blocks away. She worked as a nurse, pacing the hallways of fluorescent lights and walls so bland they promised only the chemical residue of happiness. Her white dress made her seem like an angel of mercy, but not so. She was made of patience. She was insoluble patience, born and bred to be patient, to serve others without a peep of complaint. She always seemed to be bowing her head all the time as she checked with each patient's medical clipboard. All day long in her white Thom McAn shoes she went through the motions of checking the temperatures, the blood pressures, and the IVs. The cold whiteness of nameless patients who coughed up an occasional forbidden chocolate truffle and who let loose a stench of shit onto the bed never vexed her weary face.

But I knew.

Because I knew what truly hurt her: she'd married the wrong man. My father.

Yet all that didn't matter because I was already a legend in my own mind. I was a glow coasting high on magazines, marquees, and mobs. I thought of myself glittering, like those dancers on the TV show *Solid Gold*, but only a hundred times better.

I was a real star. I felt totally blessed with the radiant warmth of my fans loving my every movement. I wanted them to fall in love with the grace of my body, to make love to me with their eyes in the dark, and to reward me with a never-ending standing ovation. Oh, yes!

In our first public performance together—I was Fred Astaire in his tuxedo to his Ginger in a white tutu speckled with sequins—I felt more alive. The fact that I misstepped once wasn't the big deal I imagined it would be.

Later in the dressing room, when we were changing into our street clothes, he stopped and looked at me. "Curt, darling. I'll tell ya—you were wonderful, wonderful!"

"Thanks."

"Of course, you were off in the last two measures."

"What do you mean?"

"Darling, you were half a beat behind."

"So? The show's over."

"No, no, no. It has to be *perfect*. Nothing more, nothing less."

"The audience has never seen anything like us. Especially you."

"Of course they haven't, darling. That's why we must be perfect. Every time."

"But we're human."

"Darling, they don't want us to be. We're nellies, remember."

"I'm not a star."

Later that night in a gay bar downtown, and after he left with some trick, I kept repeating to myself: "I'm not a star."

That was so true back in the days when I knew Dwight. He was so strong, so unique ... so *perfect*, and I was—a nothing. I was one of those products churned out every year by the dance school factories, ready to leap to any rhythm in any badly choreographed dance production. For pennies.

I was also lonely. Horribly lonely. All my friends in high school had moved away or were caught up in college. Here I was, lost in a huge room of mirrors that showed limbs spreading, stretching, and sprawling for that one more strain of sweaty perfection. But I loved the way talcum powder rose in tiny clouds from our naked feet, I loved the sinuous tights that throbbed with sore muscles aching to try again for that fluidity, I loved the tender stink that hung over the classroom as we danced—this way—then—all together now!

On my way to class the next day, Dwight caught up with me. He looked radiant, gorgeous as the mocha sun, and wore his feather earrings. I wanted to touch him, but instead I asked, "How was last night?"

Dwight just laughed. "Incredible. The shit I had to go through last night. Agggh! You should've seen the look on his face when he caught me fucking his best friend in the closet. Oooh, he was the best." He demonstrated with his hands and hips, completely oblivious to the passersby, and burst out laughing all over again. "Agggh! Oh, oh. I can't help myself, darling. Oh, oh!" He kept slapping his thighs until he was reduced to giggles. "It's so disgusting how people want to own somebody all the time. I mean, do I look like something from a pet store?" He shook his head so his feather earrings could whirl.

What was I supposed to say?

He put his hands on his hips, as in mock shock. "What? Do I look that obvious? Well, darling, I do want to be kept in a golden cage where gorgeous men can feed me credit cards—all unlimited like Amex, of course—for lunch, dinner, and a midnight snack at the latest club. I love being petted. I want to be petted by everybody. Oh. Everybody wants to take me home. It's so disgusting. You have absolutely no idea of what I have to put up with just for a night of naughty doo-doos."

I tried to ignore the looks of passersby. Some of the men looked like they wanted to pulverize us right there on the street. I kept glancing back, wondering if they were going to chase us; we couldn't hear them if they pounced on us.

Nevertheless, Dwight was carrying on as if he was perfectly safe out in broad daylight. "Agggh! Did I ever tell you about that time when I was caught in the act with this trick when the fire drill went off in his office building? He looked so cute, oh, with his shirttails flapping out like Sally Field's flying nun costume, and he looked so shocked when the fire alarm went off. I told him, 'Darling, let me climb into your asshole and I'll hide in there so nobody'll know I'm even here. I'll even take my clothes with me. Just don't fart.' Aghhh!"

Even I had to laugh at that one.

Dwight gasped to catch his breath and continued. "He looked so furious, so pissed that I just up and left with the top button of my pants hanging open so everyone could get the very filthy idea. Aggggh! Oh. I just forgot. Would you mind loaning me twenty dollars? I've got to get home and ... you know how the El is. Please. Oh, please."

I handed over a $20 bill. I still think about how much I owe him.

At the time I was living at home with my parents. Harry had gone off to college. They never asked me to move out or even to pay some rent. I just stayed in my old room. Mostly I came home to eat leftovers and sleep on the nights I didn't go to the bars with Dwight.

Days I worked downtown as a messenger, and nights I danced with Dwight. Sometimes when the classes were over, Dwight and I would stay on in that big empty room and leap all over the place, improvising all night long. Alone together in that room of mirrors I felt we had wings on our heels and feathers in our hands, as we leaped toward each other, then clutched each other into a fleeting embrace.

The gray streetlights filtered through the windows above the mirrors, and sometimes Dwight turned off the lights. There in the haze of the twilight he stood still before he began a string of movements, a flow of grace, a flutter of limbs until he became an angel arising out of the dark starkness of the streetlights. He came toward me, and without thinking, I ran toward him. We were Fred Astaire and Ginger Rogers reborn in that twilight. Then—

Everything about us always dissipated whenever I came home. Shards littered the kitchen floor, and I knew my parents had fought once again.

I ran through the house, looking for Mom and Dad, but they weren't home. I checked the garage. Their car was gone.

Where had they gone? I didn't know what to do.

I sat on the sofa, looking out the front window and waiting for them to come home.

A few minutes later it occurred to me that Mom might still be working at the hospital. I ran over and she wasn't there.

I ran back home and waited. And waited.

Well. Dad died in a bar brawl that night.

People were moved to tears at Dad's memorial service when I chose to dance instead of repeating the same old lies about how wonderful Dad was. But up there onstage I felt nothing warm for Dad, even though it was supposed to be dedicated to him. He had been so distant, a ghost threatening to strike Mom at any second for any reason, so we were never close.

Harry couldn't stop crying during the whole funeral. I thought to myself, What a spoiled brat. Now he's got no one to tell him how wonderful he is, even if he has absolutely no talent whatsoever.

I stayed on in the house with Mom. Then she sold the house and we moved to a smaller apartment.

I gave up on everything, even Dwight, and lost touch with all my friends. I quit dancing school and enrolled at Northwestern University.

One day when I was waiting in line at the campus bookstore, he came in with an older white man. They were laughing so loudly I could hear them.

I was stunned. "What are you doing here?"

Dwight giggled, as ever. "What are you doing here?"

"School."

"You're going to school? I have a boyfriend here around somewhere."

"You still dancing?"

"Me? I practice every single day, all alone. Oh, Curt. You don't know how much I've missed you."

I didn't want to look at the older man. "Me, too."

Dwight looked at his friend. "Why don't we all hit the bars right now?"

"I can't. I'm sorry. I—well." I'd never said no to him before, and I hated myself for doing that.

He simply asked, "What's your next class?"

"Economics."

His eyes lit up. "Darling, live a little. It's our duty to contribute to the GNP, you know." He began skipping gaily in circles around me while his friend tried to suppress his own laughter.

Before I knew it, I was swept back into the hurricane that was Dwight.

Before I knew it, he was borrowing money from me.

Before I knew it, we were barhopping and dancing all night long.

Before I knew it, I was completely broke.

And before I knew it, I began to feel something I hadn't quite felt before. It was hot and red and bitter. *This.*

How can I explain this without sounding like a fool? He was lovelier than before. He was a flower already in full bloom, and his easy fragrances of promises easily uprooted wafted through my nose and throughout my brain. I was forever his. I was in love like never before. I lent him everything I had until I had nothing left to lend.

One night in a corner of a dismal bar where nothing was happening, I turned to Dwight. He was finally himself, quiet and serious.

"Dwight?"

"What?"

"I really must ... tell you something."

"Ooh. I like secrets."

"You know that day when I first saw you dancing?"

"Yeah. Well?"

"I've always been in love with you. Always ..."

Dwight turned very quiet. "Really? I'm sorry." He sighed and tried his best to keep his eyes fixed on mine. "Unh. I don't think it's a good idea."

"Why not?"

"Our friendship's too ... um ..."

I know I didn't hold a trace of bitterness toward him when I finished the sentence for him: "Too good to ruin like the others?"

"Darling, really. Get serious. You know I'd never do that." No longer quiet and serious, he walked to the man next to me and put his hand on his crotch. They were gone in minutes.

I went home that night and cried for all the nights we'd never sleep together.

In the beginning Dwight was a magnet for all my friends. His one-liners were legendary: "I didn't pinch your ass for nothing. I was only squeezing a pimple on your ass. Aghhh!"

So were his come-ons: "Come here, you sexy thing." He held his breath and tilted his head backward as if to say, Take me now. How could anyone resist? He was so beautiful. And never boring. Never: losing myself in him I found the Curt in me to be incredibly boring. He was a nobody, a dancer with delusions of being a legend, when Dwight was this—*this*, and more. There was no question about it. He was a star, through and through.

He told me things he'd never told anyone. Things like: he hated being deaf. He hated being able to speak and yet not lipread very well all the time. He never felt comfortable with sign language, and he was always amazed that we could understand each other's clumsy signs.

But all I remember—no, that's not true. He had this rage inside him, but we never, never talked about it.

A memory of when Dwight came by my mother's apartment one time: "Oh hi, Mom ... Yes. Dwight's here ... He's not a bad person. You've seen him dance. He's going to be a big star ... Mom. It's not what you think. He's my best friend, he's teaching me so much about dance ... Okay, okay. I'll tell him he has to tone down his clothes. But I don't care what the neighbors think ... Who cares about how much he owes me? It's none of your damn business!"

She stood there and slapped my face.

Stung, I wept, but there was not a single tear in her eyes.

———

I stayed at a friend's house for two weeks. Then his roommate moved out with his lover on the North Side, and I moved my stuff in. I paid the rent and my share of the bills on time. Seriously.

One night Dwight, near tears, appeared suddenly on my doorstep. He had a knapsack covered with tiny pins from gay pride marches past. He also had two suitcases.

"What's wrong?"

"I got thrown out."

"What happened?"

"I couldn't pay the rent."

"Why not?"

"Well, there were ... things."

I gave him a bitter look. "I don't need a charity case."

"But you love me."

"Is that how you see me? A bed, a bank, and a bottle of fun?"

"Please. Please. Oh, please. I'll just go out of my mind if you turn me away!"

"I have to talk with my roommate."

Of course. He was supposed to stay in my room for a week or so until he found a place of his own. Of course. When he took over the bathroom, he had overstayed his welcome. My roommate demanded that he move out.

"What's the matter with you guys? I'm only trying to look pretty," Dwight said.

My roommate gave me a warning look and left for work.

"Fine," I said. "But I need to shower. I have to go to work."

"Curt, why must you work? It's so boring."

"Then move out and find another sugar daddy."

"Oh, hush," Dwight said. "Hush. Don't be so angry with me."

"Let's talk about this some other time."

Of course.

I didn't see him all that day and all night. But the next morning I found him in my living room with a complete stranger on his sleeping bag. The stranger looked like a gym-bred hustler on his way down with drugs.

I kicked Dwight. "Hey. Dwight? Get him outta here."

He sat up, disoriented, and realized where he was. He stood up, pulled up his trick, and puts his arm around him. "Darling, meet my new lover."

He stared at his trick for a moment.

"John."

"Oh, yes. John. Isn't that nice? It's John."

As I shook John's hand, I noticed how beautifully sculpted his body was; he was definitely fodder for fantasy. But I couldn't stop staring at the puncture spots where his veins stood out.

Dwight giggled. "Ahh. He has a beautiful body, don't you think?" His hand traveled down to John's groin. "This looks like nothing now, but it's a great toy."

John pushed Dwight's hand away.

"Hey. Ain't nothin' to be embarrassed about." He broke into laughter. "Aggghhh! You know what Sam—I mean, John—said to me last night? He said, 'I like Tootsie Rolls.'"

John was already picking up his clothes and putting them on.

"Wait. You're not leaving."

When the door closed, Dwight turned to me. "You still love me, don't you?"

That I couldn't answer.

The most surprising thing happened to me. I got a huge scholarship for the Joseph Holmes School of Dance, plus two thousand dollars for anything I wanted. Dwight never got anything. We met up in the hallway between classes.

"You what? Oh, darling! That's wonderful!" He gave me a hug.

"Thank you."

"Darling, you and I have been such good friends for so long, we ought to do something about that money. We should celebrate."

"What?" I knew what was coming, but he knew that I had time before my next class.

"Don't play games with me. You know."

"You want to borrow two thousand dollars?"

"No, no, darling. You know that's not what I meant."

"I owe my mother a lot of money."

"Oh, you can always pay her back anytime."

"You borrowed the money I borrowed from her."

"What's the matter with you? Darling, money was made for spending."

"No. I want you out of my sight right now."

"Let's vamoose to New York City."

I dropped my jaw. "What?"

He was already in a trance: "We can try out for Alvin Ailey ..."

"Who's paying your way?"

"Oh, Curt. I'm your dearest friend."

I walked off. I was in no mental state to attend my next class, which was jazz dancing.

He pulled my arm and forced me to look at him. "Why are you so mean to me?" His eyes were deadlocked on mine. "Is it because you love me so?"

I don't think I used my voice at all when I said, "Yes." I was damned, and damned if I didn't.

"Then stop hurting my feelings."

Of course: off we went, flying from the O'Hare to the JFK. He insisted on going to Manhattan by limo. It cost me a hundred dollars, but somehow seeing him point out the most absurd things and making me laugh so hard made it—damn it.

Every time I think about my money he'd spent without even working for it, I get so angry. I was working in a shitty job, but I was dancing in a good school. I wanted a real apartment of my own and a real life where I didn't have to feel so boxed in.

We auditioned for Alvin Ailey. We both got in. We couldn't believe our luck, and in the Howard Johnson motel above Times Square, we kept jumping around. We even trampolined on the beds, clapping. Finally someone banged the bottom of our door, and we stopped.

We couldn't stop laughing for a long time after that. Finally, when Dwight stopped gasping from laughter, he turned to me. "Let's move here. How much you got?"

"I can't leave Chicago just like that."

"But you said you love it here!"

"I do. But ..."

"Wake up and smell the coffee, darling. How many offers from Ailey are you going to get? Chicago's too small for someone like you. You've always known that."

"But ..."

"Please? Please. Oh, please." He was kneeling before me.

"No."

I told the Alvin Ailey people that I couldn't accept their offer.

Dwight said yes, but one hour before I was due to leave the hotel for the airport, he asked me for more money.

"No." I picked up my suitcase.

"Please." He threw up his hands. "Oh, screw it. I'll go with you."

When we returned to Chicago, I had only sixty-seven dollars left, and I had to lie to Dwight that I was completely broke.

I gave my mother sixty dollars and wept into my room. I didn't have the heart to tell her I won the scholarship in the first place.

In time Dwight was thrown out of his new dance class—

"Don't you think I'm good, really good?"—

The director of the new dance company he worked for dropped him—

"I'm so sorry that you feel you have to ... you know, when you've said that I was the most talented dancer you've ever worked with. Oh, please ..."—

He was fired from his job teaching independent living skills on the South Side—

"I'm really sorry that I was so late again. The El was taking so long to come that I just had to get off there and walked all the way here ..."—

He'd used up all his money—

"Darling, guess what? I've taken all of my money out of the bank, and I've got only five dollars left. Where should we go?"—

His roommates had thrown him out on the street—

"Oh, you guys. It's not my fault if so many of them want to come home with me. I don't like to hurt anyone's feelings, so I just ... Please. Please. I'll be good, I promise. I swear to God that I'll be a real angel if you'd just let me stay for one more month. I just need to find another job ..."—

Then he came right up to me after my class. "I'm leaving Chicago. New York, here I come!"

"You're moving to New York?"

"Are you coming?" Dwight looked into my eyes.

"I haven't even thought about it," I said.

"Well, I'm going."

"When?"

"Saturday. Are you coming with me?"

"Wait. Wait," I said. "You don't have any money."

"I don't care."

"You will care."

"Can I borrow fifty dollars from you? Please?"

I said nothing. I had to be strong.

"Why do you have to be so mean to me? I mean, sweetheart, this isn't like you to turn against one of your dearest friends. Darling, just think of us in New York. We don't have to put up with that narrow-minded choreographer of yours and never do all those awful numbers ever again. Darling, I know you. I know you want to let loose your legs and really move through space and time to places where no dancer's ever gone ... Please?"

It was the longest moment of my life. "No."

"Why? Chicago's not the best city for dancing. You know that."

"I'm just not ready."

"The hell you're not. Look at your dance company. They can't even do a decent Baby Elephant Walk. You're a star, damn it, and you know it. In New York we can have a real dance company of our own. Darling, we'd be rich and famous and travel all over the world and do only the numbers we like. Please? Come fly away with me."

"New York's very expensive."

"Doesn't matter if you wanna be a star. Curt, you're the It Girl they're looking for. Even Ailey wanted you."

"They wanted you too."

"Doesn't matter. Are you coming?"

"No." That no was a little easier.

"When are you moving to New York?"

"I don't want to."

"Don't lie to me. I saw how your face lit up when you saw all those buildings and all those beautiful men and all those theaters and ... Darling, don't let me down."

"One year."

"What?"

"I'll move to New York in one year."

"Fine." He walked off, and before he turned to leave, he waved to me. "*Au revoir*."

In the year Dwight was away, I rediscovered myself. I found the old Curt taking root once again like a tree.

I quit Northwestern University, and I went back to dance school. I felt stronger each day when I gave up worrying about hiding my money inside my dirty socks inside my shoes after dance class because I knew he'd be there, always waiting.

The friends I lost because of him came back.

The dance companies who once avoided me because of his reputation suddenly came around and asked me to join as a special guest. I joined the Hubbard Street Dance Company, and suddenly I was featured in the *Tribune*.

I felt more at home with myself, working hard every night. It was—I don't know how to describe it—so wonderful to find myself after all those years.

It wasn't long before rumors about him trickled back to me. First, he was homeless for two weeks. Then he was fired again. Then he found a rich boyfriend. Then he was thrown out of his apartment. And so on ...

But I didn't call him. He left messages on my machine, and my mother was always put off by the whining in his voice.

As much as I'd loved him, I knew I had to shut the door on that part of my life. Dreams of the sheer bliss on his face whenever he danced haunted me every night as my scholarship was renewed, which was a big deal at my dance school. Almost no one got that scholarship twice in a row.

Oh, I knew I was *somebody*.

But Dwight was so wrong about me. See, I didn't really want to be a dancing superstar. I wanted more than anything to be me, the same old Curtis Higgs who was happy to work with people he knew and to keep on dancing.

I didn't want New York. I wanted Chicago, and I had the city at my feet. Agents from all over came calling to see if I could audition for this or that high-profile role for some Gregory Hines show on Broadway, but I said no to every single one of them ...

Damn it, I still loved him!

Finally, when the Joyce Theater in New York offered me an opportunity to choreograph a show, I said yes. Truth was, I missed Dwight like hell. There was no other deaf dancer who really understood me as an artist.

When I arrived at my host's loft in SoHo, I was shocked to find Dwight sitting in front of the lobby. "What are you doing here?"

He was strangely cold. "Waiting for you. A friend of mine told me you would be staying here."

"What's the matter?"

"I'm lonely."

"Well, I don't know if I can invite you in. My friend's waiting for me."

"So you've become somebody. Just like you've always wanted."

"Thanks, but ... look, let me go in and talk to my friend, okay?"

He stared dismally at me. "I haven't slept in a real house for three days."

"For God's sake, why?"

"I couldn't pay the rent."

I brought in my suitcases. Of course, my host didn't want him in his place. I told him that I'd be back in a minute.

Dwight was indignant. "What? My reputation's good as gold."

"He once loaned you money. Does that sound familiar?"

"Darling, I do pay my bills. When I have the money."

"I'm sorry. You can't stay with us."

"You betrayed me."

"I did not."

"Yes, you did."

I almost wanted to push him and kick him to the ground. "No. You betrayed yourself. You have nothing—absolutely nothing—to guide your life."

"Then give me a rich boyfriend."

"You haven't kept any for longer than two months."

"Watch me." He strutted off, and I went back inside. I didn't know why then, but I was shaking so much that my host made me some tea.

At the Joyce Theater I had problems with my dancers. What I didn't want to admit to myself was that I was a terrible choreographer. I just couldn't choreograph worth anything. I was only a dancer who needed someone to tell me where, what, how, why, and when to put my legs, and I became magic.

The show was a flop. A big belly flop.

I didn't care anymore.

By then, Dwight had found a rich lover in Brooklyn. The funny thing about this guy was that he worked as a cat groomer for rich people in Manhattan.

After the savage but accurate review in the *New York Times*, Dwight called me to invite me to stay on in New York for a week.

Of course. That week stretched to three months of ... I've used the word "hell," but it wasn't exactly that. It was, well, fun.

We went to bars, shops, and, oh ...

I lived with Dwight and his cat groomer, and I found a job working as a file clerk for a law firm. Oh, I didn't care.

I joined the Alvin Ailey Dance Theater Company, and I felt so much at home with them. It was so wonderful to be told what to do with my body, and to find so much freedom in someone else's vision onstage.

Dwight fought every inch of the way to get into the Alvin Ailey, but he lost.

What he didn't want to admit was that the world of dance is really a small one, and stories about him had traveled quicker than lightning.

Dwight spent more and more time away from his lover. I knew he was afraid to be tied down in any way, and I knew he was spending what little money he had on bars and bathhouses. And I knew his lover wanted me more than he wanted Dwight.

His lover and I did it. I was so surprised and shocked that we'd even done it. The sex was lovely, but we didn't do it again.

That morning Dwight called me at work. He was hysterical because his lover had just thrown him out of his apartment; he'd had found Dwight having sex with another "rich" man in their living room. They hadn't heard him come in.

This time I chose not to help him.

I went back to Chicago.

I thought I'd never see him again. Then one night, at a major benefit for the Mark Morris Group in New York, I saw him.

He was standing way in the back, and his hair looked really different. His features were harsher and yet more brittle. His eyes ... Something was lost.

I almost lost the timing of my entrance onstage, but I knew he couldn't conquer what I had conquered. Whenever I appeared on the stage, I owned it. My limbs were naked as the need to be loved by a group of people willing to pay me back for the time and energy and money I'd invested in my own body.

This: nothing but my own soul.

———

After the show, we hugged without saying another word.

I had won. I'd finally won the battle over my soul. *This*. I was no longer in a treeless country where nothing but charity cases could take root. The soil was no longer soft and paltry, but in the country where I finally staked my claim, the loam was sweet and cushioned my feet whenever I made a leap too fast and too high. The grass was green as the small amounts of money that came to my house and eventually paid off all my debts, the fruits sweet as promises kept, and the river cold and pure as the bubble of new job offers rose ...

Across the river I saw where I used to live, and then I saw the rocky ridge. Then I saw him. Him. Not Dwight, really. But a scary thought came into my mind. A truly horrifying thought: Dwight was evil itself. Poison. He had a beautiful body, and the leaps he made from one rock to another closer to me were breathtakingly perfect. Oh, but I had to have him. The apples he gave me were brown and rotting cores of poverty and misery. Yet, with nothing in my hands, I looked down to my feet and did the only thing they were good at. They danced. Dwight was evil, and I was a hare ensnared in his fingers.

Oh, how I fell to the earth, and I landed on the other side of the river. The sun came out regularly, and my life was as stable yet exciting as could be. I was happy. I didn't have a man in my life, but that didn't matter. I was so happy.

A dream kept recurring: Dwight and I are walking toward each other somewhere in a soot-covered street of warehouses, but he is limping, ready to collapse. I run to catch him, but it's always too late.

Then I heard from a dancer friend of mine: Dwight had indeed died.

I had abandoned him. I left him standing in a country even more barren than here. I was his Old Man Oak, and I didn't even know it. He died in some anonymous hospital. What little acorns of affection I gave him, it wasn't enough. Never was.

Oh, he was my love, my love. He chose me and made me a somebody. He told me that I was, and then he went away because he knew ...

He just couldn't work hard enough. Then he got sick. Not enough food. Not enough warmth. Not enough believers ...

He was a tumbling weed lost in the corridors of New York, and I was the one who brought him down to his knees. No. It wasn't the money that broke him.

What was *this* now? What was *that* I had felt?

So much for love and friendship.

There was no memorial service for Dwight.

Late that night I sneaked into the rehearsal room where I first danced for him. I didn't turn on the lights, and somehow in the vast mirror before me, I saw his ghost in the pale moonlight and the harsh streetlight. This time he was dressed all in white, wearing a top hat, a sequined tail-jacket, and a white cane. Oh, we were no longer Astaire and Rogers. We were now equal, like Harold and Fayard Nicholas, the greatest dance team in the history of entertainment.

In the waltz that followed, I thought my heart would burst: our steps were in perfect unison, but there was no audience to applaud our orgasm of synchronicity. Who'd truly appreciate the art he'd simply given me without reservation?

Done, he touched my chin so sweetly. "I'm so sorry. Curt?"

I accepted his hand, and he spun me deep into his ethereal arms for that kiss eternal.

Night Latitudes

The night is a cat that moves and slithers through shadows. It leaves behind not a name, not a trace. Everywhere is a scene of crime, but no one knows why the yellow tape cordoning off the area is there. Just a sigh of wind tumbles between the brick walls, long battered by the decades of rain and thunder from the sea. Somewhere in the dark lurks a heart beating so quietly that one feels the world is dead, but no, the heart, the one that belongs to a man who'd long believed himself to be deformed and unmarriageable, is tapping a light tempo. It is hearing a tune long out of range, but the sliver of sun that cuts through the swirling clouds is a crystal-clear conduit.

But the man holding the heart within himself is dreaming, as always. Each day he goes to work at a large nonprofit thrift store and sorts out the unwanted junk and creates a barcode tag with prices for each item. The people who work there are nice, but he senses something's not quite right. Is it the fact that everyone working there has to give each other a superlative smile? Is it the fact that half the employees there are disabled, and therefore he should feel one of them? But he knows he isn't one of them. He likes guys, and the corporation that oversees the store doesn't have nondiscrimination against his kind built into its employment policy. No one ever talks about the night that comes and takes their breaths away while they are lulled into nothingness.

The night: what is it? It is of many particles, constantly shifting from one strand of DNA into another until a creature, fleetingly formed, looks you in the eye and disappears so quickly you have to wonder if you'd been hallucinating. But sleep itself is a hallucinatory drug. Dreams, usually fragmented and ready to shatter, flicker. Sometimes a memory, a cherished one, will play a long interlude between mashups of images that would never cohere in reality but make perfect sense in the dream theater inside one's head.

He feels for the two pillows next to him. Still there. The pillows do not a man make, but he aches to have a boyfriend unashamed of being seen with him in public. Back when he could walk, he once stood tall and wide enough that friends begged him to dress up as the giant lumberjack Paul Bunyan one Halloween. His outfit that night was a huge hit. Sitting in his wheelchair, he is still unused to his height of under five feet. No one pays him any attention when he tries to make his way through crowds. Before the accident, he'd thought nothing of standing proudly in the afternoon sun, chugging down one big cup of beer and carrying on with his buddies in the back patio of Exile. He knew he wasn't a smart guy like most guys he knew, but he had done all right for himself, considering that he had only a high school diploma. He did one factory job after another and hung out with the gals and guys in the lunchroom, but the accident changed all that. He had to learn a new foreign language laden with ugly-sounding idioms: "physical therapy," "vocational rehabilitation," and "smile, and the world will smile with you!" Yeah, right.

The night is when he can remove his mask of fake smiles and set it on his bedside table. Closing his eyes, he tries to remember what it was like to walk, run, dance, fuck, but everything is shrouded in the fog. Shadows vignette the sharp corners of buildings and boxes still left on the dock. The waves hum. In the distance a lighthouse swings its bat through the fog, but it disappears into silence. He dreams of meeting a man, perhaps someone like Captain Ahab, whose meandering story he'd read out of boredom during the early days of recovery in the hospital, the one who swore revenge on the whale that tore off his lower leg and who was forced to wear a prosthesis made of whalebone, waiting in the alcove of a kerosene-lit streetlamp for him. Ahab would tell one story after another of the sea, what an unforgiving bitch it was, and yet how unexpectedly kind it could be at times. When the flame finally gives out at dawn, Ahab would lift the man up to his feet and enclose him in a chest-crushing hug as they deep-tongued each other. He longs for that feeling of oneness with another man. He is tired of the gameplaying online, but the night is different for each person. For some, it is a dungeon waiting to be filled with moans and screams; for others, it is a booth in a lonely 24/7 diner where two people couldn't stop talking for fear of losing the power they were holding over the dark outside their windows. But most people long to hear whispers that filled the cloud of desire between two faces hovering near each other's lips.

Each morning he soaps all over himself and aims the shower nozzle to rinse the suds away. He hates how age and gravity has ballooned his belly. When the accident happened, he had a slight belly that was hardly noticeable since he had such a massive frame. No matter how he has tried to stick to his nutritionist-approved diet, he couldn't resist his favorite soda. He knows it is bad for him, but he just couldn't quit its particular flavor percolating all over his tongue. He is grateful that his bear friends don't mind the size of his belly so much, and most of them didn't move away or give him looks when he enters the bar. Things are still different, though; it's as if the air had changed, and everyone wants to do the right thing. A number of them had dated him or tricked with him in the past so they couldn't simply pretend that he wasn't there. He suspects that they'd probably talked among themselves about him and what a terrible thing it was to end up like that and what a brave man he was to be out and about. The first time after the accident was hard. Everyone had always greeted him with a loud "Woof!" when he proudly stripped down to his waist. But it wasn't so easy to peel off his shirt that time. He even practiced in front of his mirror to see what was the most natural way to take it off without looking clumsy in his chair. He settled for a flannel shirt that he left exposed all the down to the top of his belly. He is happy when his buddies cop a feel of his furry pectorals while hugging him. Sometimes one will drop a hint for a sexual encore, and he obliges, and always at his place as it's fully accessible. But no one ever leaves the bar with him. Their departures are always separate.

In the shadows that fill every gap of light leaking into his bedroom, he cannot see the chair nestled next to his bed. The ceiling is black and starless. His cock, aching, leaking, points upward. There in the skies he imagines Ahab's peg leg pounding the deck, causing the dark skies to hair-crack with lightning and thunder. His long locks would whip his face and beard but never his piercing eyes as he twists and plods toward him, holding onto the railing as his ship Pequod lurches in the roiling waves. When their bodies finally meet, surges of electricity crackles afire between their groins. Together their deformities would meld as one, much like roots spiraling out of the ground to create a gnarly trunk of tree, much like how conjoined twins would think and move as one, as they twist and turn and spear that damn whale no matter what. Together they would be the ferocious giant that neither could be alone.

At the oversized thrift store where he works, the fluorescent lights that overhang the lonely merchandise, no longer having the patina of newness but of age and abuse, make him long for the end of each day so he could go back into the furry arms of night. There he would rest his eyes and dream of the man who would be tough enough not to care what others thought of him as he bent down to kiss his man's lips in public. He wouldn't care if others asked him out right whether he had a wheelchair fetish (*nope, not at all, I fell for him as a person, I mean, look at him, isn't he sexy as hell?*), if he was a disability devotee (*he's my first disabled guy and I'm 52 so nope, I don't think so*), if he was the top in their relationship (*man, that's so personal, why do you even care?*). His man would always stand next to him, his oversized hand never leaving his shoulder, never forgetting his presence even as others fall into the habit of seeing him as just scenery, as they carried on with their happy hour buddies. No matter what they did, they wouldn't seek refuge in the dark. Their bodies together would radiate a brilliant light no matter the storms that swirled around them; each other would remain the lighthouse that cut through the tempests the way back home. This is how he falls asleep, and awakens with the urge to cry. But he doesn't. It's not because he feels that he must be a stoic and brave man; the urge to cry is the same as the rage of frustration. What else could he do? He'd done all what his doctors and therapists recommended, which did help to a large degree, but it did not alter the reality of his legs. Feeling sorry for himself isn't an option. The line between prolonged self-pity and suicide is easily crossed.

He knows a number of bears who were educated and book-smart. He likes them all right, but their talk always intimidates him. He hates the feeling that he has to be witty and knowledgeable about everything in order to keep up with them. He is a simple man in a wheelchair. That is pretty much all one needs to understand about him. He wants a husband, still a strange word to utter out loud. He wants to sit next to someone and hold his hand and watch reality TV shows and game shows and big action movies. They would talk shit about this and that, and things would be all right. It wouldn't be a big deal to get himself ready for sex as the chair would be a non-issue for his husband. There, in the warm tenderness of a match lit between their bodies, they would float together on the clouds of orgasm. The stupid whale and the damn Pequod could crash against the rocks and splinter into jagged planks and deep pools of blood for all he cared.

Late one Friday night, when dreams aren't enough to keep him tranquilized, he goes online. In the gleam of screen, he searches gay dating sites for disabled men. There are a few, but preliminary scans of each site makes it clear that not many disabled gay or bisexual men have created profiles. The paucity depresses him. He knows he isn't the only disabled gay man in the world, but he often feels that way. He decides to create a

Craigslist ad headlined with AM I THE ONLY CRIPPLE AROUND HERE? He writes: *i'm tired of guys pretending i'm not there with my wheelchair. do you feel that way too? hit me up.* A few hours later, when he wakes up, he finds an email response that contained only a phone number. He calls, expecting a conversation filled with awkward pauses. Instead he found the voice to be deep and casual. He doesn't sound too educated. He laughs easily. They make plans to meet in a coffeehouse with a wheelchair-accessible bathroom later that afternoon. It is such a relief not to explain his disability in advance.

The stranger in the chair is there before he arrived. He had tried not to hope for a beefy man, the stormkeeper of his dreams, and the stranger isn't. He is a slender man in his 40s who needed the use of a wheelchair half the time; otherwise he uses a walker. Their table has no chairs so there is no need to deal with the logistics of pushing the chair over to the next table. He coasts right up to the table and introduces himself. He couldn't believe how natural it feels to shake hands with another disabled man, knowing full well that he is gay too, and how effortless it is to talk about their before-and-after lives. As afternoon melts into evening, they gaze at each other during a sudden lull in their conversation. "All I wanna know is," he says, "who's got the better bathroom?"

They crack up.

A moment later he says, and he does try to say it ever so casually as if it is something he says every day: "Um, wanna come over to my place and check out my bathroom?"

"Sure." Not even a nervous laugh. Wow. The stranger was interested!

As these two men, having long sailed the seven seas with their own Pequods prior to trading their war stories, navigate the choppy waters of trying to wheel down together on the sidewalk toward his apartment building as more and more young people flit around them on their way to the bars, sardine together in the elevator car, and slide off their plankchairs into the ocean of his bed, the night holds its breath as it compasses how the two men, tentatively at first and then aggressively, kiss each other. The night soon weeps a sky full of stars at the sight of their nakedness illuminating with their hands and tongues the maiden voyage of each other's bodies.

You Feel Beautiful

In the time that it takes Ted to return from the bathroom, Michael looks around Ted's tiny apartment near Dupont Circle. The walls are almost bare, the furniture's arrangement is almost geometric, the pile of unopened bills and junk mail sits neatly in the center of the kitchen table. He looks at the red-and-white cane with its folded silver joints near the foyer; he still feels warm from Ted placing his fingers lightly over his hands in ASL. When they first met in the bar, a sweaty intimacy arose from feeling each other's hands as they talked. Michael had been wondering all evening about the color of Ted's eyes behind his orange glasses when Ted asked in ASL, "Me-feel your face?"

He looked about himself. "O-k."

Michael stood still as Ted's fingers felt the contours of his face. "Not-know you nice b-e-a-r-d."

"Thank-you."

"You-must v-e-r-y handsome. How old you?"

"Twenty."

"W-o-w-w-o-w. You lonesome tonight?"

Michael was not sure how to answer, but he knew he wanted to feel more of those fingers touching his face; it was amazingly comforting not to worry about being poked in the eyes. "No. Not really ..."

In the time that it took Ted to unleash his cane into a long stick and to swing lightly from side to side in front of his feet, Michael felt Ted's intermittent squeezing of his elbow as Michael led him along outside. It was a strange

71

but wonderful sensation to feel so needed, and so trusted to keep him away from the cars whizzing by in the hot August night. "Turn left 16 Street four doors over big pink house."

"We-arrive."

"You w-o-n-d-e-r-f-u-l guide. Can't believe you never guided deaf-blind man before." His hand reaches out in the air until it finds Michael's face. "B-e-a-u-t-i-f-u-l you."

Michael is still not sure what to do, lying naked on Ted's bed and watching Ted walk from the bathroom to the bed. How does one let a deaf-blind man know what Michael wants in bed? His bedroom eyes had always made things easy.

Ted feels for the edge of his bed and sits down in his underwear. "Where you?" Michael reaches over and guides Ted's hand down there, and is surprised when he smiles. "Not-yet. S-a-v-e best last."

"Not understand."

"Me show-you." Ted's fingers are feeling their way down to Michael's toes. "Tell me color h-a-i-r here."

Michael sits up and looks at them with a Martian's eyes as he signs into Ted's left hand. "Not-yet b-l-a-c-k, will change soon." He watches Ted change expressions from happy to concern to chuckle. "What you do-do?"

"Know your body must. Color your skin?"

"White."

"No. People say they're white, not-true, they really p-e-a-c-h. You p-e-a-c-h? Look. Have f-r-e-c-k-l-e-s. L-o-o-k." Ted points to his shoulders. "Not white."

"Same. Have. F-r-e-c-k-l-e-s." He takes Ted's hands to his face, to his shoulders, and to certain parts of his arms and legs. "M-o-l-e back have also."

"Where?"

"You-search." Michael feels the light strokes all over his back until Ted finds the mole.

"T-i-t, color what?"

He looks down at his chest. "A-little pink, t-a-n most."

"Exact p-i-n-k where?" He guides Ted's tongue with his index finger and finds it licking both his finger and nipple. "Taste like orange s-h-e-r-b-e-t."

He tries not to laugh. "Like ice-cream?"

"Of-course! But orange s-h-e-r-b-e-t?"

"Favorite ice-cream me." Ted grins.

"O-h. Thank-you."

"Color what?" Ted rubs Michael's chest hair.

"Black."

Ted feels Michael's wavy hair. "Color what?"

"B-l-o-n-d. No, s-t-r-a-w-b-e-r-r-y strawberry b-l-o-n-d. Dark red little yellow."

Ted smiles and kisses him on the forehead. "You-smell n-i-c-e. You-use S-e-l-s-u-n B-l-u-e?"

"How you know?"

"Experience." Ted chuckles.

"Color what?" He nudges his nose into Michael's beard.

"Red. Both orange-red same-as old fire."

"Same-as hot-dogs cooked too-long?"

Michael laughs.

"You-tremble n-i-c-e laugh. You-t-i-c-k-l-i-s-h?"

"Yes. But—"

"I-know. Won't." He smiles. "Me-same t-i-c-k-l-i-s-h. Color what?" He strokes Michael's pubic hair. "H-a-i-r you-have lot. Me-like."

"Why question-question? Go-ahead fun."

"Go-ahead what?"

"You-know." Michael guides Ted back onto the bed. His mouth zeroes into the space between Ted's thighs.

After his economics class the next day, Michael takes a pair of jeans off the rack at Hecht's and steps into the dressing room. He has never looked at his naked body closely in a full-length mirror at how skinny he really is, but he'd rather not look. Besides, why should he when he had to look at it every day? Yet he can't stop thinking of Ted's comment: "You-feel beautiful."

Leaving his jeans on the hook, Michael stares at himself in the full-length mirror. He stares so hard it does not register in him that his standing naked behind two shutter doors is quite ludicrous.

"Feel-feel beautiful?" He closes his eyes and lets his fingers wander as lightly as Ted would all over his chest and feels those ridges and indentations of his body. He wishes to describe to Ted just how b-e-a-u-t-i-f-u-l he feels right now.

Lazarus

Hearing his alarm clock ring at eight, Robert opens his eyes, and as he reaches crookedly to turn it off, he reminds himself, as he does every morning, that he will take each moment as it comes, and that he must take today one minute at a time.

He is relieved to find that he doesn't feel either cold or warm. In fact, he has been having a lucky streak of waking up and finding his body comfortable with its temperature; today would be the fourth in a row. He must remember to tell Eric, his best friend who's also learned as much as he could on the subject of multiple sclerosis, about this unexpected blessing. Robert pushes down his blankets and tries to move his legs.

Stiff.

"Nothing new," he mutters. He longs to have a man willing enough to love him in spite of his sickness and to massage the soreness of inertia out of his legs.

He thinks consciously, *Move. Yes. Up. Now!*

His knees reach slowly toward the ceiling, and they collapse onto his bed. He must try again to fend off that threat of a lingering stiffness—he must move his legs, even if it means being fatigued for half of the day.

The next attempt finds him finally lifting his entire legs up in the air—back in the days of disco music and poppers and setting trends with his haircuts of models gracing covers of *GQ* and other fashion magazines—all that had been so easy, so natural, so pleasurable, and now this. Some days he didn't have enough strength to open and close a pair of scissors!

Sometimes it felt as if the old witty partyboy Robert had splintered and died in a hundred different ways, and this stiffness only reminded him of the new Robert he had yet to forge out of his awkward reality. Oh, how he hated being stiff, and yet so weak at the same time ... He wishes more than anything for just one more morning when he could wake up with gusto, and to think nothing of standing up in his bathtub to shower.

Give me a gorgeous man with a big heart to love me and I'll revive better than Lazarus, he'd pleaded with God more than once. But that his prayers went unanswered is nothing new.

As he turns to sit on the edge of his bed, he lets the weight of his legs hang. He rubs his knees a little, as if to revive their circulation, before tottering the familiar path to the bathroom.

Robert's thighs lean against the edge of his bathroom sink, his face and neck already lathered with cream enhanced with aloe vera and lanolin, and Robert stares at himself in the mirror with a razor in his hand, wondering just how much his MS would affect him today.

As a hairstylist, he'd thought nothing of lathering some of his customers and shaving them. He remembers, with a strong tinge of embarrassment, his refrain from those days: why had they been so afraid of shaving when they were very much capable of doing it themselves? He stares at his hand holding the razor in the mirror, thankful he hadn't trembled yet. He brings it under the gushing faucet, and slides it down one cheek: still, no trembling yet. He is even more thankful for having such a smooth complexion.

He brings the razor under the faucet, shaking it again, and then up again, down against his cheek. He smiles at himself, an image of a blond Santa Claus and points at the mirror as if to say, "Gotcha this time, kid!"

Outside Robert stands, wobbles almost, and leans his cane against the brick wall. He imagines himself to be a photographer of sorts, and tries to see the cane in some artistic form or representation of beauty. Passersby on Greenwich Avenue do not even stop to look at it.

Nothing comes into his head, but the desire to have enough strength to snap it in half over his knee, and walk away as if nothing truly happened.

But it is only a few minutes before he really wobbles in standing up, so back to the cane he totters. He feels slightly dizzy from not holding on to anything, and as much as he hates using a cane in public, he needs it.

He continues dreaming of a man who wouldn't mind being his walking crutch, encouraging him not to use his cane again and to be more like everyone else in the neighborhood. He'd walk, arm in arm, and naturally for his lover would feel inspired enough with a lively spring in his own walk. Why, he'd feel like running sometimes!

He grapples a little with his cane—the most hated object of his entire universe, and yet the most necessary—before walking further down Greenwich Avenue. He only had limited energy for his barest shopping errands.

His thin hand rests on his embattled cane, his knees sore after so much walking. Had he actually gone past three storefronts—that many steps?—without stopping. No. That is too dangerous where his muscles were concerned; they sometimes worked together naturally, spasmodically, or simply not at all.

It had been six years since he'd spent two weeks in the hospital for testing to learn the medical name for that peculiar thread running throughout his life: the occasional blackout (when he was ten, he collapsed on the sidewalk near the post office and heard voices: "Dunno what it could be but he needs help," "Call an ambulance!", "Oh, Bobby, you poor boy"), his frustrating depth perception (he crossed the street many times only to find an oncoming car screeching tires when he'd thought it was a good distance away), and those frightening attacks of double vision (he'd never found those cross-eyed jokes funny). Since then he'd progressed to resigning from his job as a famous hairstylist to fighting the curse of fatigue from minute to minute, from step to step.

Yes. He must rest one more minute. Again. He closes his eyes and feels more sharply the dizzying sensation of having spun around and around and around on the sidewalk although he knows he'd only ambled forward, toward his apartment building.

As he blinks open his eyes, a convertible packed with kids rolls by. One of the boys squeal, "Look! That fag can't even swish!" while its passengers break into sharp raucous giggly laughter as they sped through a red light.

His knees lose its near buoyancy so he lets his weight fall forward on his cane. Yes. He will endure one more step, and the next ... After all, the 1990s promise to be a new decade.

Robert feels odd, having come into the card shop around the corner from his apartment to get something for an acquaintance who'd just come down with Kaposi's sarcoma, in seeing how the wheelchair's spokes sparkled in the too-brightly-lit aisle of the card shop around the corner from his apartment. The man in the wheelchair looks younger than his forty years, his temples not yet thinning and his smooth forehead unmarred by the occasional consternated lines. He is pointing to a loud-colored birthday card in the upper rows from which a Korean cashier plucks for him to peruse.

The stranger's throat feels dry. He looks up at Robert, and catches the look of embarrassment rippling across his face. Was Robert cruising him, or was he simply mortified in seeing a cripple in his wheelchair up close? He looks again at Robert, and thinks, *He is kinda cute. Can't be more than 35 years old, his blond hair looks so good on him, I wonder what he's got.*

He nods to the woman. "I think I'll take this one."

She returns to the back where she'd been opening boxes of new Thanksgiving cards, and he pushes himself past Robert. "Hullo." As he waits for Robert to reply, he grasps his own mistake: the look on Robert's face was nothing but an unadulterated white fear.

He looks down on his card and mumbles, "Guess I should take this now." He's seen the same look elsewhere so it's a good thing he also understands.

Robert is a little fatigued from that trip to the card shop, but on his bed, he feels safer. He fixes his head atop two pillows and opens his legs apart; he's already taken off his underwear easing his ass on a towel—one never knew when he'd lose control of his bowels—and opened a *Colt Studio Presents* magazine to a picture of a leatherman moaning while being fellated.

Robert's penis is still flaccid, so he strokes it some but it doesn't feel a part of himself. *Shit.*

An hour ago he'd felt quite distinctly the stream of urine, he was positive of that, and yesterday morning he awoke with a raging erection, and he cursed himself all day then for not having his last date—*had it been four months already?*—see that so Don would believe him that yes, he was capable of having erections and fucking any man he wanted.

He sighs, giving up all pretense of masturbating like he'd always done in the days before he was diagnosed and closed his eyes. He falls asleep, thinking, *Why do I even bother.*

He still remembers too clearly those nights he'd spent dancing feverishly hotly and madly, ready for the next encounter in the backroom or the inevitable balcony, and inhaling poppers and one of those tokes he bummed from one of his friends.

He was the most popular haircutter in Studio 54, making sure after hours in his bathroom that he looked precisely perfect with his outfit and a round of preliminary drugs for that right state of mind, as he hailed down one cab after another to one party after another. It was glorious, frenzied, mad. He had so much energy, so much life, so much passion that he supposed it had to end abruptly.

After the diagnosis, those calls with choice gossip stopped coming, the wild parties went on without him, the late afternoon visits dwindled.

Some mornings he wept bitterly, wishing his goddamn hands and arms would just stop curling up the way they did every morning, and wishing he wouldn't have to go to the bathroom every so often. What had he done to deserve this? His friends were still out there, living: feeling high, drunk, and grand from fucking ass like there was no tomorrow.

He still dreams of himself somehow raised from the dead and being allowed again the miracle of dancing like John Travolta in *Saturday Night Fever*. The stiffness of his muscles would be all dispelled into the blinking strobe light, splintering into prisms brighter than anything he'd ever done and all those eyes adoring him all the more for it.

Kicks

Some mornings when the mailroom's not so busy, I teach my boss Renee some more signs. Her signing's not too bad for a hearing person; she's not afraid to use her face, especially when we talk about the guys in our lives, those we know and those we wish to have known. She's the only one who knows how much I want to be a famous model, something better than those *Playguy* pictures Davy had posed in the nude for; but I've never told her about him, even if he once was the only deaf model here in New York. I haven't seen him in quite some time since he was carried off to St. Vincent's. It's hard to believe it's already 1983, and I'm twenty-four years old.

So we watch each other's diets, making sure that she doesn't gain any more than what she has on now, and that I don't get flab on my stomach. I pick up rich guys a lot; it doesn't hurt that a whole lot of them think deaf guys are great in bed. Some of them worship the floor I walk on, and they shower gifts on me. What they don't know—or if they do, they don't acknowledge it—is that I'm theirs only for a time, but not for life. There's always someone else better, and with more money, waiting.

On my first day of working here, she had just tossed her banana peel over the mountainous stacks on her desk into her wastebasket when I came in, unsure of who was Renee and where was she. She pointed to the chair beside her desk and leaned forward a little; I was surprised at how easy it was to lipread her. "Let Mother tell you something. I'm going to keep you here as long as I can because I want you to check out these boys for me." She leaned closer to me, and as she pointed to the traffic below her window, I smelled the fetid banana in her whisper. "I want to know how big they get."

79

Her conspiratorial looks often remind me of Davy when I first moved to New York a few years ago after quitting tech school upstate in Rochester. We'd met earlier that evening at a party, and later that night he invited me to the Palladium. I was very turned on by his fluttering around me; it was as if he was a moth attracted to the flame of my body. To this day I don't understand why he went off with some other guy, quite out of the blue: I suppose he had a bigger basket than I did.

From the window Renee and I make comments on the guys walking in and out of the lobby below, and when everything else drops to a standstill in the mailroom, we trade myths and true-story anecdotes about the guys we've slept with. She's had only four guys in her entire life, so I end up telling her a lot more than I should.

We look out the window again, and a man with a trimmed full beard from the eighth floor walks briskly into our building. "Such a pity."

"Married, right?"

"Yes. And for the third time." She holds up her *W* hand; she is the kind of signer that will always confuse the letter *W* with the number three.

"How do you know?"

"When you've been in here as long as I have, you pick up on those things. It's fun, kind of a game, just to figure out things. I do that when I'm bored." I laugh at her drollness, and we laugh even harder when she points out that she calls her best friend in California every day. Using her work phone to make long-distance calls is her biggest vice.

It's 11:52. She knows I like my lunch hours to be long because—well, why not? I leave with her telling me to be careful with the boys out there.

Here in Midtown a lot of cute guys go from office to deli, and from deli to drugstore, and from drugstore to office: somehow this is more exciting than bars. There are no counters to lean against, and everyone is in constant motion. And so many of them are my type: close-cropped haircuts, clean-shaven chins, matching jacket and trousers, silk ties, Italian designer shoes, and smart watches. I have yet to meet a deaf guy who knows how to dress as well as I do.

Of course the ones with money are the thing: they never seem to know how to say no to pretty boys like me. I tell them I don't have credit cards or a condo to my name, so they help pay my rent, take me out to all the new restaurants, and buy me the latest clothes. I never tell my deaf friends about this; they'd think I'm cheap. Besides they always complain about the number of older hearing guys more willing to learn sign language compared to younger guys. Some of them are a little old, but at least they know how to spend money.

So for today I go south to the deli near Grand Central Station. I'm never that particular about delis, so I look for a short waiting line. I join it for Renee's order before I decide where to walk next. My eyes wander from street to line, storefront to corner, and businessman to ...

The Guy.

He stands three places in front of me, and all my thoughts converge suddenly on his face. His brown eyes are bright as amber, his moustache outline his thin upper lip but show off his lower lip's slight pout, and his jaw is so smoothly shaven I want to brush the one freckle off below his short sideburn. The creamy darkness on his face shows how thick his beard can be. His aviator's leather jacket shelter from the February cold his white shirt and navy blue tie, and his blue chinos show snugness around his hips. I wonder how many pounds he can benchpress.

While the paunchy man churls his lips at the woman in front of The Guy, who can't decide on the cheeses she wants, I see The Guy fidget. His feet shift weight from one to the other, and his lips purse impatiently.

I cannot look at anything or anyone else; I may never see him again. I accumulate all his tiny, unconscious gestures like lint on a wet finger; with each one I fall for, they are never enough to satisfy me. I think about the color of his nipples. When he speaks, I try to lipread him from the side.

"Ham ... rye ..."

What is he saying? I watch him drum his fingers on the counter as the surly man in his dirty apron slaps a cheddar slice atop the ham, its fat stripped clean.

Moving to the register, The Guy takes out his leather wallet, its edges whitened with age. As he removes a twenty, I see in the fold of his wallet no credit cards, only a New Jersey driver's license and a plastic stack of pictures. The woman at the counter gives him bills and change.

A minute later I order, "Ham on rye." I do not explain when Renee complains. The Guy must remain my secret; she knows too much about me already.

At the subway station I join the usual jam of people waiting to take the train downtown, weaving around women with smudged white Reeboks, striped terry socks over nylon stockings, duckhead umbrellas and Danielle Steel library books, toward the front end of my train. I stand among men in their beige overcoats, serious hats and heavy maroon leather briefcases; not one of them returns my glances. They never care to go anywhere but home.

I look around at the ever-growing clusters of people, and I glance at a tall man. He's wearing a new motorcycle jacket, its waist belt left unbuckled; his pectorals tense and sigh within his Gucci t-shirt. He must be one of those Brooklyn stallions who lives for the body, a real Marlon Brando type.

I move closer.

He looks up at me. Disgust dribbles all over his face: is it my pearl earring or are my eyes so obvious?

I shrug and continue reading my *Village Voice*. I think about The Guy again and wonder what he must be thinking—now—on his way home: does he have a Guy too on his mind? Probably not. It's possible that he has just married, and is absorbed in his own thoughts as most people on their way home seem to be. I wonder often what they think of—kids? mortgage payments? dinner plans? None of these possibilities belongs to me.

At last the train arrives but it is too full even to squeeze in, so I stand back to wait for the next one.

I look to my left; he has stood back too. I stare—for the hell of it—at him; after all, he can't avoid me as his eyes search for the next train.

I give a slight smile when I lift my chin slightly sideways. He aims his eyes past mine. I turn to see if the next train is mine. The wind whooshes from the other end; it's the uptown local. He seems to grunt.

I move even closer, blending into a cluster when he is not looking. I keep close to the back of the cluster, hoping that he will turn around and wonder where I've gone.

Now I am only a few feet away from him.

Our train comes slowly, packed like a can of sardines. I step into the half-foot-square space left behind him on the train; the subway doors close. He turns around to see who is behind him: his eyes spit disgust into mine. I try not to look too closely at the few lines on his supple neck. A lot of bull-faced guys have the softest necks.

As the train lurches forward, I smell the fading waves of impotent perfumes, *The New York Post*, and buttered popcorn. I glance down at the stallion's ass, and with a nonchalant expression, I let the back of my hand brush against it. He feels very solid. He shifts a little. I contemplate refolding my *Voice*. Then he looks up at me with vicious eyes.

A woman on one side of me moves, her elbow jarring into my back now and then. She tries to keep her bag on her shoulder but the straps seem very slippery; they are a cheap imitation red leather.

The train rocks before slowing down, and I bump into him. He braces his hand against the ceiling as I bend down to pick up my *Voice*, but he kicks it further away. I look up, about to ask just what the fuck why, only to find his eyes daring me to.

I decide not to bother with the *Voice*, and a smirk creeps onto The Bastard's face.

Well, he hasn't gotten my message ...

The train lets out some people, and heaves once more, downtown toward Astor Place and Bowling Green. My mind is so filled with a blank anger that the next time the doors open, I push him onto the platform just when the doors are about to close. I smile at him. I even lean down a little into the windows to wave back as he curses.

Others look at me, but they do not say anything.

Later that night I get a call from Alan, a mutual friend, of Davy's condition. He wants to know whether I will visit Davy or not. I don't know: they are not a family I'd choose.

I tell him on my TTY machine: I DONT KNOW IM BUSY RIGHT NOW.

The only thing I leave out in my story to Renee is what a hunk The Bastard really was. She thinks I'm such a terrific storyteller with my face and gestures, and it always seems she can never stop laughing about the silliest details. If she passes me on the way to the restroom, she breaks into giggles that make her breasts move like jello.

Sometimes the other mailroom boys ask with their faces why she is laughing so loudly in there. I shrug.

I am surprised to see The Bastard again at the subway station three days later. He has on the same jacket, and I happen to be wearing the same coat.

Today work was easy; there wasn't as much mail to cart around, and Renee stayed mostly out. And whenever she was in, she'd mimic her boss The Executive Slut as if she is Carol Channing: "Yes, I understand that you'd like your severance pay immediately, but you will have to wait out front until the check is ready. What was your last name again, please?" I know every word she says because she writes that kind of thing down on paper. She does it because she doesn't like it if I'm the only one there who's not laughing with the other guys. Renee says The Executive Slut had to sleep with the vice president—she calls him The One With No Dick At All—in order to be promoted way above three people who'd been there much longer than she was. So The Executive Slut she is.

As The Bastard swerves toward me, I wander aimlessly, as if I do not recognize him. Only in New York could I behave any way I want and not have to feel guilty.

He suddenly jabs me in my chest and says, "You don't touch guys like that!"

I sign, "Sorry-sorry, me not understand talk-talk."

"The hell you don't!" He kicks one side of my shin with his Zodiac cowboy boot, and saunters off coolly.

I limp after him and hide behind a beam; it seems those beams have those fresh NEW PAINT signs every other day.

I wait for our train to come. He lags behind a taller and older businessman getting on, but I do not slip aboard. While The Bastard struggles to squeeze in, I kick him in the ass. I am surprised at how soft it feels.

His face bangs against the businessman's back, and the older man's elbow jabs The Bastard's face in reflex. As the train doors close, he steams, alternating between curses at me and apologies to the disgruntled businessman. I notice the blackness of his middle fingernail as I flutter my eyelashes and blow him a kiss.

When his train finally leaves, I realize the throbbing pain in my shin.

I rest my leg on the sofa and watch a rerun of *Cosby*. I think of how nice it would be to be a part of a rich, deaf family, and to have a rich, deaf lover, perhaps someone like The Guy. I fall asleep to the throbbing ache of such dreams.

Everyone comes in late this morning; it must be one of those Mondays. I tell Renee about last Friday, which of course sends her off into a heaven of hysterics. Even The Executive Slut's glare cannot quiet her.

I wonder again whether I should tell her about The Guy, or about Davy dying, or about wanting to be a part of some family.

My excuse to The Executive Slut—that I bumped into my bed this morning—sends Renee off to the restroom.

———

The next day I wander painfully—my leg still hurting somewhat—up and down Lexington Avenue to see if The Guy would ever return. I monitor the deli from a variety of viewpoints, different corners and nearby gourmet stands, as if I am waiting for someone to meet me.

Finally he arrives with a dark scowl plastered on his face. As he walks past, he looks up as if something in the window behind me has distracted him.

I look down and berate myself instantly for turning away. As he joins the line outside the deli, he gives me a look of puzzlement.

The lunch hour traffic eats away at my patience. I look at my watch every twenty seconds, then back at the deli window where I can see him.

The Guy steps out finally with a white bag of what I imagine to be something like a ham and cheddar sandwich on rye, no seeds. As he walks back, I think of how badly I need to piss; but he stops in front of me and says, "Is something the matter?"

I mouth my words slowly and carefully. "No. I'm fine."

He gives me the same look as before—I am used to this kind of reaction from those who expect me to speak—and continues north on Lexington. I blend into the crowds, following him to the corner of 47th and Lexington where I loiter. He walks east past Third Avenue; I'll cover that next time.

I return to work early. Renee says, "Scott, are you all right?"

I shake my head. "No. I'm tired of working here."

Renee's hands fly to her hips. "How do you think I feel after working here for twenty-six years?" She leaves when the UPS delivery man shows up with his clipboard.

The next morning The Bastard is poised outside the token booth at the subway station. I recognize him from the escalator, and I steel myself against the pain of my limp. A cop with a panda's stomach stands watch near the exit doors; I am relieved to see him there, even if he is ugly with a stalk-like pimple on one side of his reddish neck.

People mill about me as I walk toward the street entrance. I do not give The Bastard any glint of recognition as I follow closely behind a woman in an ermine coat.

As I walk past the cop, The Bastard yells, "That's the queer I was tellin' you ..." At least that is what I think I've heard, but my ears are hardly 100% accurate.

I continue walking on ahead. There is a sudden tremor of feet running after me. I turn to find the cop looking at me, and then at The Bastard. I sign, "Sorry-sorry, me deaf. Wrong-wrong?"

"He kicked me on the train." I indicate lipreading is a difficult art, which is true for most people anyhow.

"What?" I make my voice crack like a scratchy record and sign at the same time. "I kicked you on the train? Yes I did, you touched my ass, you fags make me sick!" I storm off, forgetting the sharp pain in my leg.

Renee thinks this even funnier, and The Executive Slut gives me a look suggesting I should be quarantined with Renee. My boss has taken to calling me Smart-Ass Scott.

Alan calls me to invite me to a small get-together brunch with his friends after visiting Davy together. I think how nice it would be, but I know these people. They never talk about anything else but who has died, who might get it next, and how they'd handle it if they got it. I say on my TTY machine: IM SORRY BUT IM REALLY BUSY.

I stay away from the deli for two days, but by Friday I have to see The Guy again. The pain in my leg is almost gone, and I wander about on 47th Street. Half a block ahead is The Guy, turning south on Lexington.

I join the line in the deli without thinking whether I should or not. The Guy is six places ahead of me, but as he turns around he recognizes me. He smiles a little, but turns to stare at the menu above the counter. He leaves the deli without looking back.

A week later I see The Bastard again, this time across the street from the deli; it is slightly warmer now. With spring barely blossoming above the sidewalks and with The Guy on my mind so much, I've forgotten about The Bastard's build. People brushing by carry lunches in tiny Saks Fifth Avenue bags, strained Duane Reade plastic bags, and battered leather attachés.

As he runs up to me, his eyes burn like the sun's smoking ray in a magnifying glass, and I am a matchbook underneath. "You're not going anywhere, aren'tcha?" I can hear enough to know this is a statement.

"You are very wrong." I try to swerve around him, but he grabs my bag and takes Renee's lunch out. It is a plastic tray filled with radishes, green peppers, and other salad greens with three tiny containers of ranch dressing; she could never get enough of that stuff.

He unsnaps it open. "Now you don't. Eat!"

I pretend to be about to pour on the dressing, but I jerk it instead into his eyes. It drips like paint on his leather jacket as I leap into a run.

At Lexington and 48th, I turn left and sneak into a spacious lobby. As I pace my breathing on the escalator, I look back. Nothing.

I return to the mailroom twenty-five minutes late; I leave Renee's new salad on her counter.

Later Renee stands in front of me. "Why didn't you tell Mother you got back home?"

Sometimes I hate her way of talking; if I were hearing, I'd probably hate her even more and work elsewhere for better money.

"You found someone and you two went at it like squirrels and you just got back from his place or what?"

I give her a look of exasperation.

"I thought we got along good, you know, like good friends."

I wonder why I even bother to tell her anything.

"Scott, you're not very smart." She looks around, and in a lower voice, she says, "The Executive Slut was looking for you. Let Mother tell you something. You can't always be late. Because. If. You. Do. You. Will. Get. Fired. So take those packages up to the eleventh floor."

As I enter the down escalator at the station, I suddenly sense someone familiar behind me. The Bastard smiles with the sleeve of my jacket already in his vise. "Goin' home just now, huh?" He shoves me a little as we step off the escalator and pits me against a beam on the platform. Bystanders watch us with bored eyes as he pulls my collar against the beam.

"Fag." He turns around and notices the bystanders. "Look at this fag here—"

I ram my knee up against his basket. Yowling out in pain, he makes a move to grab me again, but I am already off. I look back, and he is bending over, the veins vivid against his neck and a hand over his crotch.

Renee will never know about this.

The next few nights I get nightmares. The Bastard has been stalking the bars with a gleaming switchblade in his hand; he finds me dancing with

The Guy, who happens to be a deaf millionaire's son so he knows signs; we've already planned a vacation in the Bahamas. The only thing left for us to do remains after the dancing: the answer that leads from the question to the bed. But The Bastard steps between us, and he rips my shirt apart with its few buttons popping. Plunging his knife into me, he whispers clearly enough: "Now, that's a lesson for you."

And then this: The Bastard hires a private investigator, who finds out where I live. With that address in hand, The Bastard goes and waits next to my mailbox in my building. There are variations of our struggle in the lobby, but the end remains the same: I die with no one else hearing my last gasps for help. I wake up early and think of any other last things I need to do short of following one of those *How to Write Your Own Will* guides.

I check the back of the new *Voice* to see if The Bastard has left any warnings there for me. There are none: it is as if I do not exist.

I sit with the *Post* spread out in front of me. I am early, and Renee doesn't even arrive until 8:30. Time passes as I force myself to read its lurid scandals all the way through.

Renee taps on my head lightly. "Was the party last night so good that you came straight to work?"

I jolt. "No ..."

"Mmm. You'll have to tell Mother what's wrong."

"No, no."

She walks around my desk and pulls me off my chair and squeezes me. I feel smothered by her soft flesh. "Now, honey, you've got Mother right here, so tell me what's wrong, mmm?"

"Please, please. Not here. Not at work."

"We can eat out for lunch."

I shake my head vehemently.

She gives me a look that means, We're in for a long day.

Yet I keep thinking of The Guy, and how he will save me from The Bastard, and how I really will have to tell someone other than Renee who thinks everything I say is funny, or has to be funny. But how can I trust another deaf person if they gossip so much in detail about Davy's sex life? And about who might've gotten it from?

I hurry so fast that I don't realize I'm right behind The Guy. It's been chilly today so it is easy to imagine his warmth. He turns around and says, "Something the matter or what?"

I shake my head in reflex, and remembering my resolution to be more upfront, I nod.

"Hey, you! The usual?" It is the churlish man again.

"Yeah." He turns back to me. "You wanna talk about it?"

"Hey, you!" The man barks at me. "What d'ya want?"

I mouth slowly and point out what I want: "Ham and cheddar on rye, no seeds." The man nods and pulls together deftly my order.

The Guy looks at me. "You just ordered the same thing as me."

"I'm sorry."

After we leave the deli, The Guy gestures his bag toward Burger King. "We can go inside there."

We clear our table of its scattered salt and torn ends of straw wrappers. He opens his bag and begins chomping away on his sandwich.

Between bites he says, "Well, eat."

"I can't."

"Why not?"

"Why do you want to listen to me?"

"Well ... it so happens that you look like you need a girl."

I shake my head and take a deep breath. "I think I'm in love with you." I feel again the rare clarity of my own speech: I feel for once as if I am hearing.

He turns red, almost coughing on his bite. "I can't understand that kind of thing, y'know what I mean?"

I nod, my lips turning tense and tight and taut.

He wraps up his sandwich and drops it back into his bag. "Sorry, pal."

I take a bite from my sandwich. Ham and cheddar tastes putrid in my mouth, and I stuff it into a trash bin.

While I finish sorting the mail for tomorrow's first delivery, I find Renee hasn't budged from her counter, still chattering away on the phone with her mother. She told me once that she'd sometimes leave long-distance cryptic messages on her friends' answering machines, and they'd either have to wait for her next call or call her themselves. "It's a game, kinda fun," she said; somehow she hasn't lost a friend yet.

When she sees me in my jacket, she waves me over and covers the receiver with her hand. "Going home now? Mother needs you here." She points to the seat beside her desk. I resign myself to watching from her window workers hurry toward the subway. Some go by very fast, even in their high heels.

A new thought chills me: what if The Bastard catches me in this window? I sit back, but I find I cannot just lean back and relax as I'd always done when we're alone. Even The Executive Slut is going home early for once. I pull my sock up; it is then Renee says, "Bye, kissy-kissy poo-poo."

She looks over. "That's a nice sock you have. What brand is it?" She writes the word BRAND down.

"That's not a brand. You ask which designer." I write the name down.

"I'm sorry, okay?" She lifts her hands in exasperation. "I don't know what else I can do. I thought if you needed help, you'd ask me ... I know it's got to be some man on your mind, and it's not fun anymore, right? You in love? Well?"

"I can't explain."

"Are you in a hurry?"

I nod.

"We can eat out if you want."

"God forbid."

"Now that sounds more like Smart Scott."

I do not even smile.

"You know I miss him. What happened?" She says this very quietly.

I head for the elevators.

Dropping a token into the turnstile, I leap down the grimy steps toward my train's platform. When I slow down, I'm amazed I should feel so free now in this place.

I look around, but The Bastard is nowhere to be seen. As I walk to the place where the front car of my train will stop, he steps out from behind a beam and pulls my collar to his chest and drags me near the wall under the grimy staircase. He slams me against it, and its hardness stings through my shoulder blades and tailbone. I feel like a floppy doll in his hands as he throttles me again. "Huh? Huh!"

I look past him to see if The Guy will ever show up. The taste of ham and cheddar on rye, no seeds, rises in my mouth.

I scream to the best of my ability, "Go ahead, fuck me all you want, I got nothing to live for!" My stomach feels queasy, ready to heave.

A look of surprise crosses his face. He walks away, past onlookers with their books and papers. I avert from their faces, watching instead a sewer rat nosing a candy wrapper. It skitters away when the train comes.

Two hours later I sit with Oscar, from among the better ones in my stable of rich men, in a pasta restaurant on West 58th Street; he is sixty years old. Although it takes him forever to get it up, he is fond of French-kissing me. When he turns amorous behind his bedroom door off Central Park West, I close my eyes and fantasize of someone else. It is the only way I can come, and they never ask. Besides, my deafness makes it hard for them to ask me those questions they want to ask the most; their inquisitive glances roll off my shoulders like piffled raindrops.

But Oscar is very nice; he knows how to put clothes together, and shops only at Barneys New York and Bergdorf Goodman; he even has his own tailor. He is not easy to lipread, but he does try to communicate with gestures and an occasional scribble on a notepad. Tonight I have ordered spinach linguini enveloped in a creamy wine sauce and a cluster of sautéed mushrooms; at twenty dollars, it had better be exquisite.

As I light another cigarette, I notice a quartet of deaf men entering and taking a larger round table near the rear; I am relieved I do not know them. They are wearing jeans, Izods, and deck shoes; their hands do not know how to talk in a well-mannered and tempered manner. As I watch their conversation, I feel ashamed that they should talk boldly about sex and how one could die from it. I know it won't be long before Davy's name will crop up. It does, and then I turn my attention to the plate before me.

Oscar speaks slowly, "Do you know them?"

I shake my head no.

That night I dream I've become an old man, wearing a toupee and plastered sideburns, in a pink Cadillac cruising the condemned warehouses of Alphabet City. Off one corner, I catch through the open door of a pool hall a group of older deaf guys talking and laughing and playing cards while two beer-gutted guys outside the doorway nudge each other, pointing to my car with their aluminum cans. The shorter one mumbles something, and they break into raucous laughter.

As I drive away, I suddenly remember I have met these two a long time ago.

Angels

This was how he wanted to be found gloriously dead: on the sidewalk, with pastel pills strewn like flower petals. His body would be blanketed with a shimmering aura. A strong beam of sunlight would break from the gray ceiling of clouds to cast a glow on his calm face. Strangers gawking at him while paramedics checked his vitals would wonder if they were witnessing a dead angel being carried away. They would recall the art of prayer, thought long lost since childhood, and bow their heads in the drizzle.

His seizures were easy to predict. The sudden taste of copper on his tongue and the tightness of his stomach were the signals he needed to lay down with his pillow, which he always carried in a backpack, and wait for the aura to pass. Once, when he felt strong enough to focus on the strangers kneeling beside him, they asked if he remembered anything during the blackout. "Angels," he said. "I remember angels." Afterward, he sometimes wondered if he had lied about seeing them, but the fact that he'd answered that way without pausing meant there had to be a kernel of truth somewhere. His body wanted to remember, but his brain held the key to the vault of blackout memories.

Even though he was a graphic designer for an ad agency and an artist who excelled in drawing figures in his free time, he was unable to convey the angels that he'd seen. Details were maddeningly elusive. He was quite sure that they floated, but they didn't have wings. He suspected that in mankind's absence of written language and the early days of drawing, wings were added to convey the fact they floated, but that didn't mean they actually had wings. Oh, how he longed to see them again! He stood in front of his drawing table, staring off into the descending twilight.

His neurologist suggested that he try a new anticonvulsant that had been intensively tested with remarkable results. To their surprise, the number of his seizures dropped so dramatically that he would forget the last time he had one. At first he did not notice the little things: the misplacement of his pencil, the odd reappearance of a client's ad copy in a different place on his desk, the loosened shoelace on one of his sneakers. Yet these peculiarities began to snowball into sleepless nights when he found himself unable to conjure images that his clients needed. His mind was now the color of black. He tried to cast it aside and forced himself to think in mind-dizzying colors. He created and combined a mix of vector shapes and colors on the computer. More and more of his clients demanded another pass, and again, until the CEO had to take him aside and ask what was wrong. He couldn't explain his lingering malaise. He was never sure if it was because of the stress of his employment situation or because of the new pill.

One evening he met a man named John, a financial analyst, at a talk about the history of religion. They had happened to sit next to each other and introduced themselves. Afterward they went out for pizza and talked about mankind's persistent need for a holy man to appear and solve their problems. "There is no God," John said. "Only angels." He was surprised. It had been a long time since anyone talked about angels. "Why do you say that?" John reached across the table and stroked his forearm. "I see angels everywhere, and you're one of them." Later that night, when they made love, they felt as if not themselves at all. Their nakedness belonged to someone they knew, but they had forgotten each other's name. The taste of skin, nipple, and penis was a feast of ephemera, only to enter the permanent archive of memory and smell. Spent, they collapsed on John's bed and turned to each other. It was as if they were seeing each other for the first time. "I think I love you," he said. He had boyfriends in the past, but none of them lasted beyond a year. John was different. He was indeed the perfect man sent straight down from the heavens.

Now that he had taken a medical leave of absence from his job, his new psychiatrist suggested that he try an antidepressant. Nothing changed until a few weeks later. He felt strangely detached from the people around him when he walked the street between his apartment and the grocery store. He felt dishonest when he swiped his credit card. Did the card truly belong to him? Was that really his name? When he signed the receipt without much thought, he stopped and looked at his signature. Had he become a forger now? When he boiled water for pasta, the sound of the fierce bubbling so entranced him that he forgot he was supposed to dump in the fusilli. When John came home to find him standing in front of the oven, he turned off the stovetop. "Honey, what's wrong?" He snuggled back against John. "Please hold me and don't let me fly away." He had begun to dream that he was an angel himself. He stared at himself in the mirror and did not see evidence of a halo, but he was surely destined to float among the people milling in the mall half a mile away where he would dispense scrips containing pithy messages.

Days passed. His babble about angels coming down from the mountain turned more incoherent. John found his psychiatrist's number and explained the situation. "Stop the medication right now, and bring him in on Friday." John, not knowing that his boyfriend was an epileptic, took away both the antidepressant and anticonvulsant. Two days later John awoke early when his boyfriend's erection prodded his leg. They made animal love, grunting without joy. A good amount of pain was involved, but not too much that they lost sight of their ultimate goal to ejaculate. Afterward, John showered and left for another day of work, leaving him sleeping contentedly on the bed. The taste of copper abruptly flared up on his tongue. His stomach seemed ready to cramp. He suddenly opened his eyes, rolled over to his back, and waited. As he shook, he tried to focus on truly seeing what he thought he had been seeing all those years, but he blacked out and fell into a deep sleep.

He began drawing again. He felt alive, a curious feeling. He no longer worried about the accuracy of his angels. Their bodies were white on white with a soft smudge of gray to give a little definition. Their faces were left blank. The outlines of wings were sketched in off-white, but barely so. He chose a midnight blue chalk for the background which he smudged carefully to give the angels some depth. This he drew over and over again until he had a sheaf of them. He would tell John the truth about himself and the angels. Sometimes when he finished a drawing, he didn't know whether he should pray. It had been so long since he'd felt the hands of strangers on his body in the wake of a seizure. Many epileptics feared for their bodies when in presence of those who didn't know how to deal with a convulsing person, but knowing that he could count on seeing angels during the blackouts gave him a perverse faith in come what may.

John didn't know what to say at first when his boyfriend confessed his condition. "I feel like you're a different person now. Why did you hide it from me?" He tried to explain the anticonvulsant, but John wasn't interested; he had just spotted the drawings of angels, which were exquisitely beautiful. "I thought you didn't believe in angels," John said. "Oh, I do. Just can never prove their existence, but I feel them inside me when I black out." John stared at him. "Really? Well, you know what? I think we're done here." John gathered up his things and walked out. Not knowing what else to do, he headed for bed. Later, when he awakened, he found the bedroom dim in the late afternoon light. There, floating above him, was a brilliance casting a warm glow like a candle. No wings, he'd noted with relish. Its presence evaporated, leaving behind gray shadows.

He put on his coat and boots, and headed outside. The drizzle lent a twinkling shine to the parked cars and the pavement. The traffic on his street had quieted down for the evening. He wasn't sure where John lived. Hadn't John mentioned something about living on Circle Street and Fork Avenue? He walked east toward Fork and cursed himself for not thinking to bring along his smartphone where he could consult a map online. His fingers began to feel numb. The top of his ears began to feel the bite of cold. His knees seemed to stiffen with every step. How was this possible? It wasn't even winter. The neon that pumped the letters of GABE'S PUB glowed from across the street. Maybe he should go inside and ask where Circle Street was. He was shivering, anyhow. As he crossed Fork, he suddenly tasted copper. He hurried to the sidewalk in front of the bar, but it was too late for him to pull open the door. He stumbled and blacked out. There, in the echo chambers of his brain, he shouted to John, "Come back, please!" Exhausted, he commanded his brain: "Kill me now." He was not aware of the paramedics checking his vitals. He was simply dreaming of being found gloriously dead.

Amidst a soft hum of machinery and the elastic footsteps of nurses moving about, he was startled to find a woman in a white lab coat peering at him. Her eyes were full of concern. "Are you all right?" He said, "The sun's in my face." She glanced behind herself. "Oh! Lemme fix that." She closed the curtains. "Are you all right?" He nodded again and closed his eyes to pray. If he survived this, he would reveal to everyone his true self and how no one needed to be afraid. He would become a messenger of hope.

A Crip Fairy Tale

Born with osteogenesis imperfecta, Sebastian would learn over and over again the brittleness of his bones. His parents, both born into great wealth and unfortunately made rotten by it, were so horrified that they wanted to give him away for adoption. Grandparents from both sides of the family intervened, saying that they would be disowned if that happened: "A child isn't like a toy you could take back to the store." The boy grew up with a lingering sense of never being wanted, especially when his parents were around; his nanny and chauffeur were much kinder. He adored his four grandparents, though. Sometimes they jokingly fought among themselves over who would have the honor of paying for the many books that he wanted and the upgrades for the expensive powerchair that he needed. All he had to do was to make them laugh. He never thought he was funny, but their chortles assured him otherwise.

In college he discovered that his rapier wit, honed by the writings of Oscar Wilde and Quentin Crisp, attracted his kind of men: slim, clean-shaven, and well-dressed. He was astonished that they wanted to have sex with him. Wasn't he supposed to be a freak?

He knew how to make everyone laugh. Sometimes he made them laugh so hard they'd fall off their chairs and wipe away their tears. He held court in the cafeteria every day, and many students had found him so entertaining that they knew to come a bit early in order to grab a good seat for lunch.

Sebastian learned to gauge the mixed signals of interest and hesitation on the faces of men he'd found attractive. He whispered when they happened to be alone together: "I'm not little where it counts. Just pointing out the obvious."

97

Their double takes made him chuckle. He liked feeling powerful.

Questions then clouded their faces. How does one have sex with a little person?

He said, "Don't you worry."

He took charge once they were alone in his room. He did not want to be cradled like a baby. He was a man. Strangers on the street still baby-talked to him. He always retorted, "Since when does a baby have a beard?"

Sebastian hated the question that lingered in the air right after their orgasms, though: should he stay with Sebastian for a cuddle, or just leave? Sometimes the oddness of his body so frightened them that it would be weeks before he saw them again.

Yet a slightly younger man in particular kept coming back for more. Edmund majored in Victorian literature, preferred vintage opera recordings, reread his favorite P. G. Wodehouse novels, and hated cellphones. A hardcore Anglophile, he wore suits reminiscent of the Edwardian era.

They fell in love.

Edmund learned to ignore the gasps of disgust when he held his boyfriend's hand in public. "What are you looking at? He's *my* Prince Charming!"

Sebastian decided to try writing a comedy for the student playwright competition. His winning entry became a sold-out stage hit. By then he knew he was destined to write dialogue. Having bitchy characters fling bon mots at each other with gleeful abandon was so much fun!

After graduation, Sebastian and Edmund moved in together. Finding the right apartment with an elevator and a fully accessible bathroom had taken a while.

Edmund went on to graduate school. He eventually became regarded as a brilliant, if slightly eccentric, professor of literature. The difficulty of achieving his A's was the stuff of legend.

Sebastian continued to write comedies for local theater companies. His grandparents attended every premiere and last performance of his shows.

It was not long before Hollywood and network television came calling, but he chose to stay put. It was easier to discuss script changes via email and log online to confirm the latest direct deposits in his banking account.

Did Sebastian and Edmund get married? Of course, they did.

Happy endings are everywhere if you know where to look.

Of-Course

Everyone loved watching Chip Burns interpret in ASL onstage. How could they not? He was tall with a slender physique honed in Rye's Gym, the most exclusive health club in the city. He chose his black shirts very well: not too loose, but not too tight; just tight enough to reveal the contours of his muscles when he signed. Long regarded as one of the best interpreters in the city, he easily commanded high rates.

Men ached for him from a distance. They regarded him as an A-lister who got into parties that included only buff men. But he'd never felt entirely comfortable in their company. He enjoyed drinking beer and talking with the guys, but most of them seemed more interested in working out and hooking up. No one would've surmised that he used to be a gawky teenager who'd been bullied one time too many. He fled his alcoholic home as soon as he could after high school graduation, and set about transforming himself into a muscular he-man at the university gym. He met Todd Waynon, a deaf man who had been working out for a few years, and that was how he'd fallen into the language. He was very much attracted to Todd, but he was straight. He had wanted to look buff enough to attract the ladies. Chip went on to study ASL.

One day, when he was 35 years old, Chip tripped down the stairs.

Even though Ben Loggins had grown up in the same city as Chip did, Ben never saw him interpret. He had been outfitted with cochlear implants since he was a baby, and the implants were successful enough to enable him to master speech clear enough to be understood by most people. He had taken speech therapy all his life and sat in the front row of all his classes. He never told anyone how, even though he clearly benefited from the implants, he sometimes felt strange in having the magnetic receivers on the back of his head. He knew that kids sometimes starred at them and a few of them asked him what they were. He explained how they worked, and they inevitably said, "Oh." They never returned.

He grew up believing that he would always be alone.

His parents shed tears of joy when he graduated from high school. It was as if they weren't sure their son would succeed. Why, he was quite normal, just like anyone else!

On his first day of classes at Browell University, Ben spotted a handsome man. His name turned out to be Todd Waynon.

After Chip woke up in the hospital, the accident replayed in slow motion in his mind's eye. He thought he'd seen the next step below, but his vision suddenly became, for the lack of a better word, pixelated. In that moment of blurriness, he missed the next step and banged down the concrete steps head first. He never forgot that first jolt of pain that exploded in the small of his back, his shoulder, his neck, the back of his head. Then: nothing. Not even a color or a sound. He doesn't remember the rest. He would forever curse himself for not having bothered to hold onto the railing in the first place, and for having used the fire escape stairs instead of using the elevator, but he was in a hurry to beat the traffic for his next job.

He lay there unconscious for approximately an hour before the two women who found him called 911.

Everyone was frightened, afraid that he'd died, but the medics said that he had a pulse and that he would be all right. They didn't tell anyone at the scene that they were worried about paralysis.

His spinal cord was soon diagnosed as partially severed. Chip hated his wheelchair intensely, and it took him a year to make the necessary adjustments. He had to sell his inaccessible condo. He bought a smaller condo with an accessible bathroom and a kitchen that could be easily modified with a lower stove and refrigerator. He chose a neighborhood that wasn't trendy at all; he knew that his realtor, still feeling skittish around a disabled man, was lying when she said the neighborhood was up and coming, that its real estate values would increase in a year's time or so. But he didn't care. He couldn't bear the risk of being seen by his old friends and gym buddies.

In the first few weeks after his accident, he felt suicidal. He wanted to ask the nurse for cyanide pills. How could he live like this? He'd worked so hard, so fucking hard on his body. Now his days in the hospital were full with sessions with his support group, physical therapist, and occupational therapist. He was relieved not to see other ASL interpreters in the hospital. Each time he looked at himself in the mirror, he wanted to cry.

Everyone said that he was quite lucky. He had full use of his arms, and he had full bladder control, which meant he could have erections. His legs just didn't work. "That's all," his doctor said. "That's all that's not working right now."

"That's all"? It was so easy for anyone to say that. They didn't have to deal with being in a wheelchair.

Ben didn't know that Todd was deaf at first. He found the man's physique imposing. His biceps were works of art. They'd first passed each other in the hallway from classes and gave each other the barest of nods. He looked out for Todd whenever he was on campus, but his appearances were far and few. No matter. His hearing classmates never tried to make conversation with him. It was just as well. He was used to being alone.

Things changed in his second semester. When he entered the classroom for his first day of American History 102, he was struck by the sight of Todd sitting in the front row. Todd had been waiting to tactile-interpret for a deaf-blind woman while watching an ASL interpreter signing for a deaf sighted man. Ben wanted to bolt. He knew that other deaf people existed, and that they often signed. Yet he'd never felt the need to learn sign language.

The deaf people in the front row looked at him as if he was an oddity. He was accustomed to such looks, but he noticed something different. They weren't looking at him as if he was weird. He couldn't understand the question on their faces, and then it hit him. They wanted to know if he was truly one of them.

He spoke and tried to gesture at the same time: "I'm sorry, but I don't know sign language." Todd gave him a knowing smile.

What did that smile mean? Were deaf people always so mysterious?

But Ben didn't have time to ponder the question during the class. He couldn't take his eyes off the female ASL interpreter. That he couldn't really follow her at all didn't matter at all. It was just so fascinating. And of course, he kept glancing at Todd. He envied the deaf-blind woman for touching Todd's thick and nimble fingers. By the end of class, he realized how much information he'd missed from not lipreading the professor.

For the second class, he decided to sit further to the left, closer to where Todd sat, so he couldn't see the ASL interpreter as well. He needed to focus on his lipreading and take notes. That went better. He continued to sip in the sight of Todd: the sinewy forearms, the hefty shoulders, the square jaw, the intent eyes as he echoed the ASL interpreter onto the deaf-blind woman's hands.

Even though Ben had excelled in history during high school, American History 102 turned out to be extremely difficult. The subject matter was easy, but he couldn't focus on anything! By the third week, though, he was surprised when Todd himself stood up and beckoned him to come closer when the students drifted out of the classroom. By then Ben had learned the manual alphabet online, but he didn't feel entirely confident with his handshapes.

Now that they were alone in the classroom, Todd turned to Ben. He mouthed and signed slowly and clearly, and his gist was this: "I've seen you look at me all the time. I'm not gay. G. Understand? Okay. G. A. Understand? Okay. G. A. Y. Understand?"

Ben felt crushed.

But Todd wasn't finished. "I'm not scared, but there are other G. A. Y. guys out there. I know some deaf guys. I can introduce you to them, but you have to learn Sign."

Ben nodded. He didn't know what else to say. He hadn't told anyone about himself. Yes, he'd chatted anonymously online, but this was different. The hottest man on campus had seen right through him—had he been that obvious?

Todd gestured and fingerspelled, "What's your email address?"

Ben took out his notebook and wrote it down.

Todd gave him a thumb up and left.

In those dark days when autumn turned into winter and finally spring, his best friend Lila visited Chip every day. As ASL interpreters, they'd worked together, translating the script for each production at the Washburn Theater. He'd always liked her because she was really astute with her sign choices. Lila was also eternally single. She was never interested in marriage, and she was frank about her need to hook up with men now and then. She appreciated that her gay friends didn't judge her for wanting sex with various men.

She stopped by to visit with Chip whenever she could between assignments and at the end of the day. There, amidst the clatter from outside the hallways and the low buzz of television nearby, they signed to each other. Even though he could use his voice, he'd found it easier to express himself in ASL. Somehow those feelings had nothing to do with his old life, and he felt safer in not hearing his own feelings voiced. Just signing to Lila made him feel better.

Even though he could say that he was disabled and in a wheelchair, he still cringed when his therapist asked, "How do you feel about being disabled?"

The spoken word "disabled" had no connection to him whatsoever.

Two days later Ben got an email from Todd. BEN I WANT TO INTRODUCE YOU TO ERIC AND REUBEN THEY ARE DEAF STUDENTS AND THEY ARE GAY TODD. He saw their addresses in the CC: field. He didn't know what he was supposed to say to these two guys. Nonetheless, he responded, THANK YOU TODD. I LOOK FORWARD TO HEARING FROM ERIC AND REUBEN WHEN THEY ARE FREE. BEN When he clicked on SEND, he realized to his horror that he'd used the word "hearing" in his email. Would that make an unfavorable first impression on Eric and Reuben? He fretted over this all day and tried to put it out of his mind when he was in his classes.

He got a reply that afternoon. HI BEN, YOU FREE TONIGHT? WE CAN MEET 7 PM AT THE FOUNTAIN. ERIC The Fountain was the campus social center where they served beer and pizza every night.

Ten minutes later Reuben chimed in. 7 PM GOOD FOR ME TOO

Ben wrote, I CAN MEET YOU THERE TONIGHT AT 7.

He was afraid of what might happen. He had been in college for almost two semesters, and he hadn't made real friends. He did know a few of his hearing classmates, but they hadn't offered to get together at the Fountain.

Not knowing what to expect, Ben took a shower and chose a nice shirt and pants. He was at the Fountain fifteen minutes early. He wondered what Eric and Rubin looked like. He practiced his fingerspelling.

Then he spotted two young men signing together. One was tall and bearded, and the other was overweight and mustached.

Ben waved his hand when they scanned the expanse of tiny tables.

They waved and smiled as they came toward him.

The overweight guy glanced at the back of his head. He made a sign that consisted of two flat fingers indicating where the transmitter lay flat upon his scalp, held in place by the magnet in the internal receiver.

Ben nodded in acknowledgement that, yes, he had cochlear implants. The two men traded glances and sat down.

The tall one said, "Me name n-a-m-e name R-e-u-b-e-n namesign-Reuben."

Ben wasn't sure what the tall one had said, but all his years as an expert lipreader had taught him one thing: context was key to everything. He recognized the letter R on Rubin's fingers, so he'd made the assumption that the other one was Eric. He fingerspelled each word: "Nice to meet you, Reuben."

Reuben responded with rapid-fire fingerspelling: "Good fingerspelling, but not sign language."

Ben felt embarrassed by their patience in teaching him a few signs, which he had no problem absorbing, and then they'd decided to challenge him and see how many signs he could master.

He discovered that learning ASL vocabulary was easy, but he couldn't quite comprehend the grammar and syntax of ASL dialogue between Eric and Rubin.

That evening turned out to be an awakening. It was as if he had been slumbering all his life. Magic wasn't made of sounds and shadows, but of hands and sun rays illuminating everything they touched.

Word of Chip's accident spread quickly through the ASL interpreter community, the Deaf community, and the gay community. He saw what they'd posted on his Facebook page, but he didn't respond. "So sorry!" "Get well soon!" "Hope to see you when you get better." Did they truly know how bad it was? Losing the use of one's legs wasn't the same thing as having a bout of pneumonia. They absolutely had no clue!

When he was finally settled in his new home, he took a deep breath and dialed Access Providers, his favorite agency. "Hi. Is Rona there?"

"Who is this?"

"Chip Burns."

"Oh! Chip! It's been a long time. My gosh, how long has it been? A year? Are you feeling better?" His mind went blank when he tried to place the receptionist's name.

"Yes."

"Wait—hold on." A moment. "I'm transferring you to Rona now."

A soft click, then a full deep breath. "Hi, Chip. Great to hear from you!"

"Yeah, good to hear from you too."

"It's really busy today, but yes, we should get together."

A beat. "Yeah. I'd like that. Where?"

"You know where. Our favorite spot. Charms Bakery!"

He'd forgotten about that place. They served the best scones in town.

"Yeah. Which day are we—"

"Tomorrow. Is eight too early? Just that we get so busy around here."

The next morning he found himself in front of the bakery and realized to his horror that the bakery, which was a house converted into a restaurant, had three steps. No ramps anywhere. There was no way he could wheel into that place. He'd have to ask for help. He contemplated turning around and cancelling the get-together, but there she was, already striding up to him. She wore loose slacks and high-heeled boots, and the gloss of her nail polish complemented her lipstick. But there was a faltering in her gaze. "Uh ..."

"Hi. I didn't realize this place wasn't accessible so ..."

"Oh, Chip. I'm so sorry."

"Sorry about what?"

"You know."

"I just want to get back to work. I can still sign." He switched to ASL. "Fast-sign still-same. Hearing full still-same. Voice follow fast-sign still-same."

She looked like she was going to cry.

"Hey." He switched back to his voice. "It's not the end of the world. I'm ready to work."

"I'm sorry. I just ... I just can't."

"You just can't what?"

"This is ... I don't know how you do it."

"Rona? You've worked with disabled people before, so why is this a problem?"

She looked like she wanted to say something, but she stopped.

"What? Tell me."

"I can't. You know I can't say it."

"Can't say what?"

"You know."

"No, I don't."

"It's not right. I know it's not right."

"I'm not following you."

"Never mind."

"Rona."

"I'm sorry, but ... it's not going to be easy."

"What are you talking about?"

"Years ago we had someone move like you here from another city. She was very good, but we couldn't place her once deaf clients saw her. Nobody wants a disabled interpreter."

"I don't get it. Deaf people are disabled. Technically, anyway."

Rona took a deep breath. "I know. I'm sorry."

"You've got to give me work. You've seen my work. I can't believe I have to beg!"

"All right. I'll see what I can do."

He tried not to turn bitter when he didn't get a call that week, and this in a city with never enough interpreters to go around! And he was one of the best!

He emailed the other agencies in town and alerted them of his availability.

It was as if he'd become blacklisted.

Then a smaller agency called him and asked if he could be on call for urgent care assignments. It was not long before he got his first call. He nearly cried on the bus there. He'd done those emergency assignments a lifetime ago, and he never liked doing them. It involved a lot of waiting for the nurse and the doctor to return. He liked to be interpreting *something*. He couldn't believe that he had to be reduced to emergency jobs, but this was better than nothing. He knew that all hospitals, by law, had to be completely accessible. That was the one thing he liked about hospitals now.

As he wheeled into the urgent care station, the receptionist said, "What can we do for you?" She wore a white sweater over her pale blue top.

"I'm Chip Burns. I'm interpreting for Jimmy Phillips."

"Oh, no, no. You can't be an interpreter."

With a deadpan face, he signed without voice: "F-u-c-k y-o-u look-down-me think nothing interpret can't."

"Oh, um." She hadn't understood a single thing. "Okay. Um, I'll be right back." She walked to the back and closed a door.

He watched her whisper to her boss through a partially shaded window.

She returned. "I suppose we have to use you. Come this way."

He wheeled beside her down the hallway to Bay C. There, Jimmy was hooked up to an IV drip. He was in his thirties, and they'd seen each other many times before at deaf events, but it was the first time that Jimmy would be Chip's client.

Chip smiled and signed, "Hello, me C-h-i-p B-u-r-n-s namesign-Chip, your interpreter today, how you?"

Jimmy looked at him. "Wheelchair why? Happened?"

"Accident happened. Explain later. You more important. You ok?"

The job went well, or so he'd thought.

The next day the agency's president called him. "It seems that the hospital was a bit upset about us sending you there. They don't want their clients to feel uncomfortable, so I'm afraid I'll have to ..."

"I can't believe this."

That was how he ended up being a voice relay interpreter. At least no one on the videophone could see that he was a wheelchair user. He'd done VRS interpreting in the past, and he always hated the feelings of isolation produced from sitting in the same booth for hours on end.

Ben went with Eric and Reuben to bear events, where he made new deaf friends. Yet he didn't feel entirely comfortable. He enjoyed their company, but he didn't feel sexually attracted to most of them. He liked in-shape guys. When he went to the clubs with his new friends, he was agog at how buff men, usually shirtless, danced shamelessly with each other.

Sometimes he went home with a hearing guy from those clubs, but they weren't always muscular. He didn't mind. Touching another guy regardless of his body type was still a thrilling experience. Each man that he had sex with taught him, usually without words, the many ways two guys could make love to each other. He couldn't get enough of touching another guy. It was as if touching a guy made him feel much more alive. He wasn't a ghost drifting through the haunted mansion of life. He was alive, and his body affirmed that glorious reality.

By the end of his freshman year, he became a major in American Sign Language and Deaf Studies. He watched one clip after another featuring ASL poets and storytellers. He took an Introduction to Linguistics course if only to better understand how ASL was considered a language in its own right. He liked how some deaf people insisted on capitalizing "Deaf" to signify their culture. But more than anything, he hung out with them. He wasn't a sentimental person by nature, but he harbored strong feelings of tenderness and warmth toward the Deaf people he met. They were family.

When he visited with his parents, he began to realize that he never belonged to his own family. They still faced him when they talked, but when it came to conversing among themselves, he had to work harder to lipread.

One evening over dinner he finally shared what he'd hidden from them for so long: he was majoring in ASL and Deaf Studies, not Biology as they'd thought all along. His parents were aghast.

"I don't understand," Dad said. "I mean, you do know that deaf people who use sign language never get far in life, right?"

Two years before Ben would've agreed, but not any more. He was grateful that he'd done so much reading about the Deaf experience. He could defend his own people and their language.

His parents sat quietly as they listened.

Finally, Mom said, "Excuse me. I want to say something. You're like a truly different person when you talk about this ... ASL thing."

"It's not a thing. It's a language." With that, he turned off his voice. His hands exploded with grace. They sang of bliss and spewed fury as he quoted lines from ASL poems and mimicked the hilarious use of certain classifiers from his favorite ASL stories. His parents had never witnessed such passion in Ben. They didn't understand a sign, but they'd grasped that they'd lost a son in that moment.

Ben removed the implant receivers from the back of his head, slid his speech processor off his belt, and placed them on the table. He left the dining room without saying another word.

When Chip came home from the VRS center, he sometimes never knew what to do with himself in the evenings. He cursed himself for not appreciating those days when he had his legs, when he never thought twice about climbing the stairs or having to call ahead and inquire if the building had an elevator. He missed the camaraderie he'd experienced while working out at Rye's Gym. He hadn't touched his dumbbells in over a year! His body had gone to seed; hell, it was more like a bag of birdseed!

Lila still came by, but it wasn't as often as he'd liked. Much to her surprise, she had fallen in love with a businessman with an expensive taste in clothes and wine. Chip still forgave her after she tried to convince the Washburn Theater to allow him onstage so he could interpret with her. Didn't matter if she was sitting on a short stool. His wheelchair was too much of a distraction.

He'd thought many times of suing the Washburn, but he knew how the Deaf community had long tried to dissociate themselves from the disability label and reposition themselves as a linguistic community defined by ASL and its culture, so having a disabled interpreter onstage was a major public relations issue.

Chip thought often of his alcoholic father. He had never understood why anyone needed to drink so heavily, but the more he waited for the phone to ring, the more he felt the urge to go down to the liquor store on the corner and buy a case of cheap vodka. He'd just drink himself to death, just like Dad who'd died of cirrhosis. No one was calling him for a get-together. For all practical purposes, he might as well have disappeared.

Chip tried various gay dating apps, but most of the guys recognized him from his interpreting days and asked if it was true that he had become disabled. After his cursory explanation, he noticed how they'd mysteriously dropped contact. He debated whether to mention his disability upfront in his profile, but ultimately decided against it. He figured that he'd need to get back to working out. Perhaps if he were photographed just right, preferably from slightly below to hide his wheels, he'd look able-bodied. Maybe that would convince a few to overcome their queasiness enough to meet him.

Before the accident many guys had told him that he was a stud. Where were they now?

Ben graduated first in his class from Browell University. His parents never showed up to see him give the valedictorian speech in ASL. He tried his best not to feel bitter about their absence. He moved to Washington, D.C. where he earned his masters and Ph.D. degrees from Gallaudet University. Working in an ASL-only environment was so liberating. Yet he fell in love with a hearing man who didn't know ASL, but that didn't work out. Graduate school was too time-consuming. He did the hookup thing for a while, but he found the experience of sex with strangers to be alienating. It was all about the dick, and nothing to do with the guy behind the dick. Was that all there is?

Then Browell University offered him the opportunity to teach and research as part of their ASL and Deaf Studies department. The pay was much better, and the cost of living was much lower than in D.C. It proved quite a challenge to work within a hearing university since he couldn't assume that everyone used ASL. He still enjoyed his job immensely, but the moments of loneliness, which had been far and few as he'd become a workaholic, became so strong that he checked out gay dating sites. Because he was fresh meat, he got quite a few nibbles, but he was now forty-three. He didn't want another blow-and-go; he wanted a date. A *real* date. He knew all the single Deaf gay men in his city, and none of them interested him.

There was another reason why he'd left D.C. The Deaf community wasn't what it used to be. He could remember how he could count on seeing so many of his friends at Deaf events where they'd catch up with each other, but now? It seemed as if most Deaf events had become overrun with hearing interpreter students. Where had the Deaf people gone? It seemed as if they'd become too lazy to step out from behind their computer screens and look up from their mobile devices. The number of Deaf people hadn't surely changed at all. What had changed was the nature of their community. It wasn't so close-knit anymore. He too began to notice the same thing had happened to the hearing gay community. Sure, they still hung out in clubs and bars, but their numbers were anemic compared to the pre-Internet days. Didn't community matter anymore?

When Lila asked him to become the new sign coach for the Washburn Theater, he was delighted to accept the challenge of translating English into ASL. It required different skills that he rarely got to use in his own work.

Then she asked him if he'd be comfortable with using a disabled interpreter for the rehearsals.

"Sign amazing-explode?"

"Of-course."

"Then fine, problem none."

"True-biz?"

"Why not? Me grow-up cochlear-implant, people see-me f-r-e-a-k. Not surprise i-f wheelchair same him. Discriminate should? Of-course not."

Lila smiled. "Wonderful. You-two get-along fine will."

When his cellphone rang, Chip was getting ready to go out for an evening of volunteering at the local LGBT library where he sat behind the checkout desk, scanned the bar codes, and checked them out on the computer. Not much to it, really, but he enjoyed checking out the men who browsed the shelves of books and films. He was usually paired with a volunteer so he made friends that way. He'd begun to volunteer more and more around the gay community in hopes of meeting someone special, but so far his wheelchair had only intimidated everyone. "Chip?" Traffic murmured from the caller's background.

"Hey, Lila! What's up?"

"I'm running late for my next job, but I just had to tell you that our new sign coach at Washburn is very open to working with us. As in, *you* and me."

"You serious?"

"Yep. He knows about your chair. It's not an issue for him. He just wanted a good interpreter, so I recommended you. It's just for rehearsals only, though."

"Oh, thank you, thank you, thank you!"

"Anytime. I'll call you later with more details. Gotta go."

Click.

He stared at his phone. What the hell had happened? Did he actually get asked to work at the Washburn? No. Couldn't be, but she did say the word "Washburn," right? Yeah.

That evening he couldn't help grinning. He began to wonder if the Deaf man was gay, single, hot. He knew he was hoping for too much without having seen a picture of him, but he had wondered a few times about hiring an escort. He hated the thought, though, because he knew he still looked good. He had resumed working out so his upper half was rebuilt, and he had become fanatical about having his legs massaged and exercised so their muscles wouldn't atrophy. A few hookups came over for sex, but they never returned for encores. Nobody wanted a crippled boyfriend.

The following Monday morning he wheeled into Rehearsal Room B at the Washburn. He hadn't slept much in the last few days; he was that excited to be working in a theater again even though he wouldn't be interpreting the show onstage. He even spent a good quarter-hour shaving carefully, and put in an extra ten minutes of working out his arms and shoulders. He had to beef up just in case. He glanced around the room. Actors were sipping coffee and reading the script around the table. He was happy to recognize Peggy Mann, the new theater producer, there; the previous producer had resisted Lila's pleas to allow Chip back onstage. She walked over to Chip and introduced herself. "And just who are you?"

"Chip Burns. I'm an ASL interpreter." They shook hands. "Lila should be here shortly."

"Oh, yes!" Peggy began to fingerspell and sign and speak at the same time, all of which came out mangled. "I studied ASL for two years in college. But it's been a while since ... oh, I've done it again. Everyone tells me that I shouldn't sign and speak at the same time, but you know. Anyway, have you met Ben yet?"

"No, I haven't."

"Oh, he's really good. His signs are very clear. Beautiful, actually."

"That's good to know."

"Oh, there he is! I'll be right back."

Chip turned and saw a balding man with glasses and a slight belly standing by the door near the roundtable. He was holding a binder copy of the script. The stranger lit up when he saw Peggy heading his way. He was surprised to hear Ben's imperfect speech as he signed: "Good morning, Peggy! How are you doing?"

"Great. How about yourself?" Peggy tried to sign as well, but her signing was still painful to watch.

"I'm eager to get started. Where's the director?"

"She isn't here yet." She turned to a man in his 20s. "Where's Amanda?"

"Outside." He gestured holding a telephone. "Reception in this room sucks."

She turned to Ben. "Well, there's someone you need to meet."

As they walked toward him, Chip gazed up at him. He scarcely heard Peggy's voice as they shook hands. "Nice meet-you."

"Same-you." Ben grabbed a chair from nearby and planted himself in front of Chip. "Sorry me-feel bother me-look-down-on-you, eyes-looking-at-each-other-same-height-equal, better?"

Chip was astonished. Ben had signed entire sentences as if they had been condensed into single signs. Peggy was right. His signing was indeed poetic, but with none of that shoehorned feeling from trying to accommodate English on the hands.

In that moment Chip beamed and felt the spotlight, long denied him, switch on. Together they would translate themselves into something startling and yet so *of-course*.

Riverwise

It is autumn, a time of the many hues of green turning into reds, oranges, and yellows of every shade until the branches hang empty as skeletons. The sidewalks are ambushed with leaves, dried out and curled-up and crunchy. But Eddie isn't paying attention to any of this as he zips up the rest of his hoodie and puts his hands into his pockets. Afraid to forget, he has been remembering so many things.

Down to the river Eddie goes, the slither of blood shimmering inside his veins, as the shadow of trees above flicker. He had traveled this way many times before when he was growing up, but it has been years since he's walked this way. The path once familiar to him is like a map torn up into bits. Where was that plum tree, its charcoal branches so full of tough needles? Its tiny plums used to squirt under his feet when he wasn't careful. And the strange bumpy pile of dirt and grass that he had always walked around? The sea of goldenrods has been mowed down to its scrawny remains, its silt overturned. Everything is gone, but oh, how the river ahead still surges. It's no longer wide and deep as it used to be, but its burbling movement, borne of wind and weight, still calls out to Eddie.

Up close, any river looks the same. There is the water, and there is the motion caused by the well-worn contours of rocks and fallen logs hidden underneath its surface. Pull back a bit, though, and it becomes a different landscape, a different story. Sometimes there are no trees. It all depends on where the river has to go. Standing before the water, Eddie swears he'd know these shimmers of quicksilver spilling everywhere; nothing like the fine sprinkle of diamond that barely coated the fresh snow in the morning sun. The river wasn't a pond. Its waves always moved one way no matter what, and he would never recognize himself each time he peered into the water.

Growing up he never questioned why he had felt so contract-bound to the river. It wasn't too far from his father's house and the many secrets he had to swallow in order to stay alive. The river had never demanded anything of him. Its translucent skin roiled past him, but that was all. Each time when he was forced to endure yet more humiliation, another blow from his angry father, he closed his eyes and imagined himself deeply underwater like the frogs propelling themselves further away with their powerful legs.

Sometimes Eddie imagined his father was not really human at all; just a foul-breathed monster that happened to resemble a man. He walked and talked like any other man, but once the toxins of alcohol spread through his system, he turned back into his true self. His eyes were full of spite and shadow. His hands, long used to the stress and strain of turning wrenches and screwdrivers, were powerful claws. His arms and shoulders could carry two car tires on each side of his body. When he was drunk, he mumbled. No one could understand a word of what he said, but the language of fury didn't need translation. Customers speculated that when his wife died suddenly in a car accident, he had lost a few of his marbles. How else to explain his fits of temper? People who had known him growing up said he was never really a drinker, but his buddies at Tom's Tavern could be counted on to bring him home. Eddie hated those buddies because they had never told him to stop the boozing. Eddie had come to abhor the smell of whiskey. Sometimes, when his father was snoring loudly on Sunday mornings, he unscrewed the caps off the unfinished whiskey and poured some of it down the toilet. He combined a few bottles into one and hauled the empty bottles out to the trash, hoping that his father would drink less. He was careful with the amount he let pour into the toilet, though, for fear of getting caught. It didn't help that sometimes his father brought women over some nights. He had a series of girlfriends, all of whom felt the need to straighten him out, but he always broke up with them. The problem was, he was a very handsome man with brooding eyes. Women found him extraordinarily attractive in spite of his unsavory reputation. Eddie hated it when they remarked on how handsome he was like his father, and that some girl would feel so lucky to be his wife one day. How could they not see how badly he wanted to be out of that house, far away from that asshole?

In spite of his bruises and scars, he rarely looked at his own body in the mirror. The only reason his body existed, he'd come to believe, was not just because his father's sperm and his mother's egg had merged to create him but also that his father needed someone to bear the brunt of his rage at the injustices of the world. Eddie knew, without looking, how ugly his body was; would always be as long as he was throttled, beaten, punched. He longed for Mom to return from the dead. She would surely bring a warm sunlight into their home, and her radiance would be more than enough to stop his father's drinking. He would sit calmly at the table and chuckle quietly as she carried on about this or that neighbor's shenanigans while serving him and Eddie some oatmeal. That was all he remembered of her with any certainty; all other memories of her felt hallucinatory, so he was never sure if they did happen. He couldn't remember her face clearly anymore; just the frozen image of her smiling in a photograph hidden under his bed. When his father began to throttle him in the weeks following her funeral, Eddie moved his bed to the corner and slept facing the door in case he came storming in. For a long time he had nightmares about being throttled unexpectedly from behind. He was relieved that when he hit puberty and shot up fairly quickly, he had grown too big for his father to shake him so easily. The beatings didn't stop, however.

More importantly, it had been a lifetime since Eddie saw the river. He never forgot the next-to-last time he had been here. He was sobbing so hard; only that he hadn't known he would soon turn off that faucet of emotion too hard and make it nearly impossible for him to feel anything for fear of being hurt again, in the lilting shade of a willow tree. He curled up and willed himself to die, only that no snake was large enough to consume him whole. A few hours later, when he found one side of his face freshly sunburnt, he struggled to stand. He still winced from the fresh lash scars on his back, but he knew he couldn't risk getting attention. It was best to keep wearing a tight t-shirt underneath his long-sleeved shirts and wait for the scars to fade. His body has been tattooed with stripes left behind by bruises and lacerations. This was why he never showed his body in public showers or went swimming with anyone. The river, for all its benevolence, had taught him to fight back like a fish snagged on its hook, splashing about until the tenuous line broke free, bobbing down into the depths until he felt as if his lungs were ready to burst. Breaking the surface, he felt one with the river who never demanded an explanation. It just was, and he just was, and that was how it was going to be. No questions asked.

With his face feeling kettle-hot on one side, he took off his clothes and dove into the river. Its undercurrents weren't as strong as they were the day before. He was in no danger of being pulled underwater, and even if he were, he would've welcomed the chance to disappear. The jolt of cold soothed his face, and he tried to stay afloat in one spot, but it was difficult. He suddenly detected an errant flicker of motion in the woods across the river. What was it? He stayed put for fear of exposing himself to the stranger, who soon made his presence known. It was Luke, the mechanic who worked for his father. Luke was a high school dropout from three towns over, and he was eager to learn the business with the hopes of opening his own garage one day. Eddie noticed early on how Luke had kept to himself after hours in the apartment above the garage. Sometimes the TV was on, but he was mostly reading library books on setting up a new business and repairing cars and trucks. Luke figured prominently in Eddie's masturbatory fantasies. In his early twenties, Luke was slender and smooth-chested with dirty blond hair, and he was a good-natured guy who never lost his temper. He was suited for the thankless task of peacekeeper between customers and Eddie's father; but when Eddie's father was sober, he proved extraordinarily efficient with zeroing onto the source of any problem in any ailing engine and fixing it. Hence it was easy for him to take care of so many cars in any given day and make good money; he was usually the last resort for miles around who inevitably became the first resort for customers stunned by the speed of his diagnosis and resolution. Seeing that intuition in action kept Luke in awe of Eddie's father, and the fact that he felt a strong attraction to Eddie kept him close by. Though Eddie never told anyone where he went for his absences, Luke once shadowed him through the woods. He saw where Eddie went when he wasn't busy keeping the garage clean after school and trying not to incur his father's wrath. Standing there by the river, Luke didn't say a word as he gave Eddie an unabashed smile and stripped himself down to his skivvies and dove right in.

Eddie pinched his nose with his fingers and disappeared underwater. Unlike what Hollywood would want you to believe, most rivers aren't easy to see through even on a full sunny day. Its sunbeams are always shifting, hiding, reappearing. He couldn't see, and he knew the water wasn't all that completely sanitary. As much as he loved the river, he never felt comfortable with the idea of opening his eyes underwater.

Then he felt Luke's arms surround him.

At first he thought Luke was going to hurt him, but no, quite the opposite. The heat of Luke's body against his back in the middle of the bobbing coolness surrounding them aroused him.

Together they broke the surface. Eddie wasn't sure what to do, what to say, whether to turn. He had been physically hurt so much that he'd learned it was better not to resist. But Luke's arms did not try to squeeze him.

116

"I've seen you watching me," Luke whispered into his ear. "I know what you want."

He was startled to feel Luke's erection prodding his backside. He had never thought that guys could feel that way about each other.

Moments later they made tender love off the river bank as the sun dried their wet bodies. Eddie couldn't believe that one could feel loved without having to endure pain. The clouds in his eyes parted to reveal bright vistas.

When they were done, and when their panting slowed down to the same rhythm of ease and nonchalance as the river skimming by, Luke said, "You're a good guy, but your dad ..."

"Can't we run away somewhere? Please!"

Luke nodded. The way his boss had treated his own son angered him to no end. But they needed getaway money. Luke didn't have enough experience yet to open a garage of his own, but he promised to find a way. There had to be, even if he didn't have much money. That Eddie was a junior in high school never once entered his mind. After all he had dropped out of high school himself.

That night Eddie's father smelled something different about his son. He had the nose of an animal, finely tuned to the scents that mingled and lingered after people made love, but he said nothing. A few days later he caught Luke having sex with Eddie in the garage. He did not hesitate in swinging a tire jack at Luke's head. Eddie found his own nakedness covered with tributaries of blood. He wrestled and broke free of his father's hands and ran outside on the street. He was only seventeen. The small town buzzed nothing else but the scandal for months afterward, and even more so when his history of prolonged abuse was made public in the courtroom. Eddie's emotionless revelations silenced everyone, and no one knew what to say when they saw how Eddie kept his eyes fixed on the ground when he walked from his neighbor's house, where he was staying temporarily, to school and back. Truth was, Eddie couldn't stop thinking of Luke. He cringed whenever anyone touched him, even if it was accidental. His doctor noted this fact during the trial and wondered if Eddie was in danger of becoming autistic; back then no one knew much about autism so there was a lot of speculation. When Eddie wasn't off by himself at the river, he preferred to sit beside his bedroom window and stare at the sunset fade into black. He couldn't bear to feel a thing, a single emotion. Still too dangerous.

It was not long after his father was sentenced to life that Eddie felt himself break into tiny little pieces. Yes, he could finally feel safe at night when sleeping in his new room. He had always liked the Coburns so he was grateful for their agreement to be his legal guardians. Yes, Eddie could still talk and walk as always, but he felt parts of himself slipping off the walls of his insides until he was sloshing about with his guts that looked like chili swishing about in his big rubber boots. Then he heard mysterious whispers urging him to set his father's garage on fire. Then he had to convince himself that not everyone looking at him had purple-lizard eyes. He felt as if he was disappearing.

It was clear that Eddie needed professional help. It took his psychiatrist nine months to orchestrate the right mix of medications that stabilized him enough not to dwell on the paranoia lurking in his brain. A few months later when Eddie returned home at last to the Coburns, he felt strangely distant when he saw the razed lot where his father's garage once stood. He felt increasingly more like himself, but even then he still felt detached.

Eddie knew this because he couldn't get hard. His doctor had warned him that a side effect of his medications was impotence. Some nights when he forgot to take his meds he pulled out his cock and willed himself to get hard, but his body rarely cooperated with his sexual need. When he was younger, he masturbated often beside the river, fondly recalling the men he'd seen earlier that day, but it was never with the explicitness he'd experienced with Luke. The men who populated his fantasies before his breakdown were always kept at a distance. He had felt that if these men came any closer, they would surely hurt him. The memories of Luke's nakedness still flickered across the screen of his mind, but they had been imbued with a great sadness.

Eddie ended up moving to a much bigger city two hours away and living in a one-bedroom apartment in a suburb where he worked as a truck driver, delivering stacks of the city's newspaper around town. He liked the early morning hours. No one was around, and he felt safe between the fading dark and the pale hues of sunrise. Sometimes he caught a familiar stranger smiling at him, and that was more than enough to keep him feeling sated for the day. It didn't matter if the man was ugly or not. In the days before affordable broadband access became a reality, he downloaded pictures of naked men via a squealing telephone modem. He had hundreds of stills featuring impossibly perfect bodies gyrating through the motions in a variety of positions. Even though he had an occasional stiffie, he nevertheless felt inadequate when he compared the quality of his erections against theirs on the computer screen. Then he heard of new drugs designed to address erectile dysfunction. He decided to try Viagra and discovered to his dismay how strangely disconnected his erection had felt from his own body, his own emotions. He was hard as a rock, but he felt nothing down there. He didn't feel any real pleasure. Nevertheless he kept some of the blue pills in case he had sex with another guy. Later, when he was able to download videos quickly on his home computer, he felt the emptiness within himself grow even bigger from looking at the pornographic pictures of men. He couldn't figure out why this was so, for the videos were indeed hotter than the photographs he'd hoarded. But the more he watched the videos, the more he saw that there was no love, no genuine affection between these guys who performed for the camera.

Eddie turned to the personals online and felt depressed. What did he have to offer anyone now that he wasn't able to get hard on command? He wasn't interested in getting penetrated; his father, drunk with fury, had once tried to insert a broom handle up his ass one night. Sometimes Eddie still remembered those dark moments, and they occasionally popped up unexpectedly. Right then and there he had to stop whatever he was doing, and take a few deep breaths. It wasn't enough to make everything go away, but it was enough to get him through the day until he came home from work. His therapist had taught him strategies on dealing with those flares of fear, and he knew he was doing quite well, considering. He decided to post an ad online and include his picture. He didn't say anything about his sexual difficulties. He wasn't sure what he should look for. All he knew that he wanted to feel safe with another guy, like he had with Luke.

Men from near and far complimented him on his extraordinary looks. They couldn't believe that he was still single. Some of them drove a long way just to meet him. He was that good-looking, a fact that he never believed about himself. He insisted on meeting each guy in a public place, usually at a family-friendly diner by the highway twenty minutes away from home.

Each date was filled with painful awkwardness. Eddie had only one question for each guy he met: did he like to drink? He wasn't interested in dating anyone who was remotely a social drinker.

Eddie never knew what else to say while the other guy prattled on about this or that over a cup of coffee and a slice of pie. He couldn't shake the suspicion that they were salivating over him like a wolf with a slab of meat right in front of him. Maybe it was because he had been honest upfront about his lack of experience with relationships, but he felt unable to divulge anything about his mental illness. What would anyone think of him if they realized how emotionally damaged he had been? No one would surely want him if they knew how much his father had hurt him. Sometimes when they walked out of the restaurant, the guy would turn to him and say, "Hey, how about it? Wanna go somewhere and fuck?"

119

Eddie wanted so badly—oh God how he wanted it! dreamed of it!—to have sex with a guy again, but the prospect frightened him. None of the dates seemed to understand his overwhelming need to go slow; make that very, very slow. As a result, he never had sex with any of them.

In the solitude of night he thought often of the river. Even though he was living in a suburb, he hated being so close to a big city, but there weren't any jobs to be found in the small town where he grew up. He went online to search for jobs similar to the one he had that were situated in other small towns, but there was nothing. He longed to move back to a place much quieter and cheaper. His job would have to do for now.

One overcast morning, after he'd finished his last delivery for the day, he took a booth at Arnie's, a 1950s-style diner owned by a gay man. He didn't care so much for the framed glitzy posters of movie stars from Hollywood's Golden Age, but the food was good and affordable. He liked looking at the gay guys who patronized the place and wondered if anyone there would understand him at all. He had figured a long time ago that they probably wouldn't, but he still liked looking at them anyway. The waiter took his usual order, and he looked up to find a man smiling at him from the counter. His beard was salt-and-pepper, and his love handles hung over his leather belt and jeans. His t-shirt stretched across his chest to reveal his slightly droopy pectorals, and his forearms were covered with tattoos blurred from age.

When the waiter set a cup of coffee in front of Eddie and left, the heavyset man ambled over to him and held up his own cup. "Want some company?"

Eddie looked up. He had no idea that a man could seem so short when sitting and yet so tall when standing up. "Unh, sure."

Greg introduced himself and slid onto the bench opposite Eddie. He held up his coffee and said, "Good morning." He flashed a smile.

Eddie felt bashful, which he always did when a guy expressed interest. He was never sure what they wanted from him. Sometimes he hated that he was supposed to be so good-looking. There were moments when he longed to look ugly so that a guy's interest in him would be truly genuine. Eddie was too happy to let Greg to do all the talking. The more he looked at Greg, the more he found the idea of his bulk reassuring. There was a world-weary kindness in his brown eyes, and Eddie liked how he often laughed at himself in a deprecating way. He too was a truck driver, and he drove his Mack diesel along the interstate. His territory covered five states. He had been at it for twenty-five years, and he was getting real tired of it. "All these years, and for what? Look at me. The road ain't good to me." Then he whispered, "I don't mean to take the Lord's name in vain, but Jesus H. Christ, you're fucking beautiful. You know that?"

"Um, thank you."

Greg looked at him for a long moment. "We need to talk. Let's go outside."

He followed Greg, marveling at his height and stride, to the parking lot. They went to Greg's battered 4x4. "I'm gonna be direct here, okay? Guys look at me and think I'm a top, and they want me to dominate them, but the fucking truth is, I'm on antidepressants. I hate it because I can't get it up anymore, so when I look at someone like you, I feel so ..." He tried to laugh. "Well, you could say I make a great cuddle monster. If that's not enough for you, I understand. I mean, I always say I'm a bottom, but I hate getting fucked. But it's the only option I got when I want to get someone interested in me. But I need those damn pills. It's the only way I can hold down a job. But dammit, I'm just so tired of getting fucked, so ... If you don't wanna play with me, I understand. I bet you get your pick of the guys all the time, but damn it, I gotta say this—you're so fucking beautiful you can break my heart any time you want."

Eddie felt as if his own heart was about to stop, then it began beating back, hard. His chest felt as if it would burst from so much feeling, so much emotion. It had been so long. Too long!

"You okay?"

"Yeah," Eddie finally said. "Um. You got plans for today?"

"Nope. What do you have in mind?"

"Can you come with me?"

"Sure. Where are we going?"

"It's two hours away."

"Well ..."

"I wanna get naked with you," he finally rasped.

Greg chuckled. "I can deal with that." He got into Eddie's truck.

They held hands while a great silence, heavy with expectation and wonder, hung in the air. No one dared to talk, afraid to break the spell between them.

As Eddie drove, he kept glancing back at Greg's visage. He really was a handsome man. Didn't matter that he was much older or that he wasn't a conventional beauty or anything. He was just handsome, period.

Finally Eddie parked on a scruffy side road off the two-lane highway. It was fifteen minutes away from where he had grown up. The skies had cleared up by then. The early afternoon sun was strong.

"Where are we going?" Greg asked. "I'm feeling like ... What are we doing here?"

"Please. Just ... just."

Greg nodded. "Okay."

He gripped Greg's hand as they headed through the woods toward the river. There, as they stood before the shimmering waters, he turned to Greg. "I'm on meds too. Just, uh, hold me. Please."

He couldn't help but tremble in Greg's vast arms and inhale a waterfall of musk and sweat. He felt his own erection rise in his pants. Didn't matter right now if he could shoot or not, but that he was able to get hard, even if it was semi-hard, was more than enough. It had been so long that he'd felt this good. For a long time they stood there, roaming their hands all over each other's backsides and tonguing each other's faces amidst sloppy kisses, until Greg suggested that they strip naked and lie on the grass. There, they held each other fiercely as they gyrated their groins against each other, their eyes never leaving each other, for a long time. They fellated each other, but even when they became softly erect, they didn't ejaculate. Greg stopped moving for a moment and rolled his eyes suddenly. "That was fucking amazing," Greg finally said. "I felt like I was shooting stars up here in my head. Wow. Did you feel that too?"

Eddie nodded.

Afterward they went skinny-dipping. The water chilled their bones, but Greg was never far from Eddie. He insisted on holding him afloat. It was the first time Eddie began to let go of Luke from his body's memory of the river.

On their ride back to Greg's truck in Arnie's parking lot, they couldn't stop talking and laughing and feeling occasionally shy about looking so directly at each other. Eddie beamed whenever Greg sneaked a wink at him. They soon moved in together, and they couldn't stop holding hands everywhere they went. Eddie took great pleasure in overhearing strangers wondering what such a gorgeous man could possibly see in such an old fatso. Some speculated that Eddie was a chubby chaser, but he wasn't that way at all. If only they knew what an amazing and doting husband Greg was! Each night, when Greg wasn't on the road, they clung to each other as if the other would accidentally roll off their wide bed into the dark sea of nothingness.

It has been exactly one year since Greg died of a heart attack. They had been together for almost seventeen years.

Today, as Eddie stands before the river, he knows that he has to stop grieving and start giving. It is his turn to be someone's cuddle monster. He would never be ashamed of his impotence; he is still every inch a man no matter what anyone says. After all, Greg had said so. Someone out there had to be longing for a guy like him who understood his own condition. He knows that not many guys have had the rare fortune of being so unconditionally loved by another man as he had. It is time to pay it forward. He may not be tall and bulky as Greg was, but he does not need the river anymore. It is now surging inside his entire body, its waves pushing upward into his heart and throbbing outward through his veins.

The Room of My Eyes

When he entered the room of my eyes that day, something changed. It felt at first vague, but became infinitely cool, real, concrete. I felt him rustling the sheets of my bed, and I felt his fingers pressing my body softly against his. I whispered his name as he did this, and all this before he revealed to me his name. I did not have to strain my ears to hear his voice or my eyes to read his lips. When he entered the room of my eyes, I knew all that needed to be known, and yet I ached for much more. Whatever doors had been closed inside me were all flung open to his silent gaze, the flint-blue irises that made whatever words he chose to impart seem meaningless, trivial. I held my breath whenever he spoke, and my eyes swung madly on his every word. No, I knew he wasn't a god of any sort, but the power he did not know he had over me was far too gripping. I let myself drown in that clean-shaven face before me: his strong jaw, tiny pricks of freckles under his eyes, firm lips, his short blond curls, and those eyes. When I first saw him that day, I found myself exploring his eyes. It was a strange and unfamiliar room, but one in which I felt at once home. I wanted to turn boldly to him and to kiss him fully on the lips, right in front of all those strangers stranded in the elevator. I wanted to pull his body close to mine, grope through his suit the flesh he did not know he was blessed to have, and slide each of his fingertips into my mouth to let him know—*yes*. I would lick the dust from a day's work at the office accumulated on his black wingtip shoes. I wanted to trace his nipples through his freshly ironed shirt, then scorch each one with my furnace mouth. I wanted to feel my hands tremble as they traveled from his sweaty heels to his calves and to his thighs. I wanted to trace the mounds of his ass as he lay on his stomach, peacefully sleeping on my bed. I wanted to lick the sun off his shoulders. I wanted to pull open his armpits and let the nervous odor fill my senses. I wanted to kiss every sign he would try to convey on his hands: I would teach him the imprecise language of precise desire. I wanted to commit his entire body to memory so that should I ever lose my vision, I would never forget his sensuous and violent ways beneath my sheets. When he entered the room of my eyes, I did not know yet how much I wanted him. I lay there the morning after, alone as always, and suddenly found myself so hard from remembering his face, whose name I did not know until I fingerspelled the name I'd call him if I would be allowed to do so. But where was I after all in the room of *his* eyes? His name had flashed only once in my mind, and yet I couldn't be sure. He was just a man who stood next to me, saying not even a word, but having given me only that slight smile. As he waited, I saw in his eyes a restless soul, and I wanted him in my arms, to soothe him and give voice to his yearnings. I wanted to listen more carefully than ever to his voice, to that *something* which had changed irrevocably inside me, in that emptiness of my hands held open: oh, if I could, I would not feel any more the need to say something but simply rest my head on his shoulder as we stroll down the street, with our arms around each other, the two rooms of our eyes having somehow conjoined into a room larger than ourselves.

I awoke to find my dank room mottled with moss, my body covered with vines crawling and a moist dust creeping with the sun cutting a sweet swath through the musty panes. My limbs weak, I glanced to the other side of our bed, finding the man I loved gone. No trace of him: had he truly left me for a hearing man, or for dead, or had I simply dreamed up every inch of him in the room of my eyes? I struggled to get up, ignoring the thinness of my ribcage. When I lifted my head, my dizziness hurt. I closed my eyes to face the sun. The warmth soothed me. I got up, shakily but slowly, and felt even more dizzy as I tottered to the window. I leaned for a breath's rest against the moth-eaten drapes. *Damn him, where is he now?* My stomach rumbled a thunderous hunger. I opened my eyes and caught the shock of my gnarly beard in the window's reflective glint. My aching bones told me that I must've slept a year, maybe more. I touched my face, my carved-out cheekbones. *He couldn't have abandoned me—no, not like this. Damn it, he was supposed to love me!* I remembered acutely the savage beauty he gave me, and how much more to him I'd given. I pushed open the window, and a rush of warm peppermint wafted in. I looked below at the fetid moat, and to the rolling meadows beyond. Everything was a summery green, nothing like the drab and cold February when we first met, when we were desperate for a little color. In the distance I saw an army of naked men heading toward my castle. They were all on foot, carrying burlap knapsacks of food and blankets. My eyes were still unused to so much light, and the muscles around my eyes were already sore from squinting. But as the men came closer, I recognized some of them, the deaf men I always wanted to know and love ever since I began learning their language years ago. They stopped signing with each other to gaze up into my weeping eyes as the morning sun rained down on my frail shoulders. *Oh, where have they been, and for so long? And why had I been separated from them in the first place? I never got to learn their stories.* Much too hungry to think of anything else, I fell back in the stark shadows and struggled my way out of the bedroom. Each step down the winding stairs in the dark tower gave my bare soles shocks of wet iciness. In the dark flight down I recalled ghosts of all these men I'd starved for from afar, falling in love with the way their faces and hands moved, feeding an unspent volume of hope in my search for a kindred mate in my naïve days: how odd to see them again, and all naked as I'd secretly dreamed. At the bottom step, I found the huge wooden door bolted. Through a crack I saw the men signing passionately to each other on how to smash open the door with a log near the moat's edge. Their pectorals shifted so brightly with each expansive gesture, their biceps flickering with each fingerspelled word, and their mouths pursing with each grunt as they centipeded the log right at the door: the sweat on their skins glimmered their beauty, each one of them. I climbed back up the stairs, only a few steps, and watched the sunshine splinter at last the lingering darkness. The door surrendered, and the end of the log was steadied onto the threshold. I watched the shadow of a man with rangy shoulders loom larger on the wall opposite the moat, and I remembered the hearing man I loved. He once struck fear in my heart, yet this new shadow was gentle, precarious as it crossed the sagging log. Then the stranger peered into my darkness; the smattering of hair on his body glistened as if a halo. When he ferreted me out, a beastly specter against the unforgiving walls, his broad grin melted me. Tiptoeing around the splinters and rusted nails, he scooped me into his arms. I fainted, a sheer miracle against the wall of his chest fur and steady arms. *If this is heaven, I'd never want to die.*

Reawakening on the meadows what must be hours later, I discover my body enveloped in a forgotten aura. My bones are wrapped supple with muscle; my nails and beard, trimmed. Cleansed, I have been fleshed out with food; yet a strange, thrilling taste lingers in the back of my throat. As I survey their glances, I realize that I haven't merely imagined our abundant feast. They pull me up to my feet. I'm hardly surprised by their familiarity with my body, nor mine with theirs: oh, what sweet crimes they commit with their hands, interpreting perfectly the grammar of my desires! Walking among them and looking deep into each deaf man's eyes, I beg: *Translate me. Translate me into words best left unspoken on my tongue. Teach me so that I may comprehend all the body's mysteries. Fill me with travels of countries I've never heard of, with my body its only passport.* Behind them all, I see the men of whose legendary stories I've heard remnants a long time ago, and now I have connected with them in the flesh. My eyes are so diffused by tears that I can't see clearly, and my dry tongue thirsts for sweat as their eyes penetrate every pore of my body. I could've been ashes in their hands, yet they chose to salvage me, to revive. As I introduce myself with my name sign, I glance back at the castle where I'd slept for a year: now in ruins, its shadow is already creeping closer to our feet as the sun arcs west. As the men sweep me onto their path home, we swap stories as if nothing bad had ever happened. Feeling my voice freed through my hands, lonesome no longer, I feel gloriously alive, talking and laughing without worrying whether I could speak or hear. *Why hadn't anyone told me how truly wonderful life could be?* The further away we move from the castle, I see the opaque silhouette of the hearing man I once loved standing in the window of what used to be our one room up in the tower. He is alone, unable to convey with his hands the one year between us. *Oh, how could anyone be so selfish as to stay silent in the language of touch just **shouting**?* No longer his, I am forever theirs to touch, and all the heavens are mine to behold and share.

Community Building

I hobble with my cane down the crooked forest path from the Love Canopy. I've candy-striped my cane with ribbons and topped it off with a carnation corsage. I wear an old wide-brimmed hat with a price tag that says FREE sewn on. I wear a paisley-print toga that I've made myself. Everyone says I look fabulous as Gaudy Gandhi, which is my faerie name for the week. But no one gropes me amidst the flash orgies in the Love Canopy.

Radical faeries think they don't discriminate.

But they do. Oh, how they do!

Most radical faeries who've come to this retreat are too young to remember Minnie Pearl, the comedienne who sported a hat that hung the price tag of $1.98. She always was something of a huckster with her hillbilly humor, especially when she was on the TV show *Hee-Haw*. The humor was thigh-slapping oh-gosh-golly as if these strange folks were meant to be misunderstood and shrugged off with a chuckle.

But I do remember. I refuse to be called Pity Pearl.

For a long time I never wanted to be near freaks. Kids were shushed when they saw how the freaks gimped, rolled, and stuttered. Freaks were zoo animals let loose. They were all lumped together as a single species. Never mind the fact that each freak is never a generalization. Us freaks are to be avoided. After all, what little they've known of us comes from observing us at a very uncomfortable range. They can't imagine living the way we do. The question of us is a very painful one to answer.

Yet their superiority allows them to gawk at us.

Sometimes we inspire them with Internet memes that get shared on Facebook and retweeted on Twitter and reposted on Tumblr. Do these memes make us feel any better? No. We have been reduced to sight-bites designed to make able-bodied people feel better about themselves. If an armless man can change a baby's diapers, which seems like a miracle to anyone except to those who've adapted their toes as fingers, their own lives may not be so bad after all. We cripples are put on this planet to make everyone else feel better about themselves. We've seen too many people apologize for their unthinking behavior, and yet they rarely change. They figure they'll never have to deal with us again.

Even though I've got a perfectly functioning penis with plenty of love spooge for anybody who wants it, it's as if we cripples are supposed to stay asexual. No one ever asks us how we can fuck if our bodies aren't the same as theirs. No one asks if we want to date and have boyfriends. There are times when I've the urge to create a t-shirt that says, I CAN STILL WALK, with a cane below, and AND I STILL CAN COCK, with the same cane flipped upward like an erection. But I don't have enough balls to wear such a shirt in public. It's too incendiary, and I'm afraid of turning off a prospective boyfriend.

I know why we are unpopular with the cool faeries, including the ones who claim to be very accepting of everyone. It's too hard to bullshit with us.

Faeries argue with me that there is no such thing as an A-list faerie. "Everyone's different, but they're all equal," they say.

"Really? Then why do I feel like a pariah? Can't someone give me a little lovin'?"

They stare at me as if I've become too selfish for my own good. I want to remind them of what they'd shared in our heart circles over the past few days: how they'd expressed doubts about their own physical attractiveness and their fears stemming from loneliness. But we cannot refer to what we've learned in the circle. What's shared within the circle stays there.

The faeries with the more beautiful bodies are the ones who get the most sex. I should know. I've hung out in the Love Canopy and jacked off listlessly while I watched. Once in a while an older faerie will offer himself to me, and of course I'll go down on him. But is it always reciprocal? Rarely. I'm somehow too freakish for him.

I'm a confirmed masturbator. It's not what I want to be, but when you get told most insistently in so many ways that you are not desirable enough, you have to make do. I've thought about walking about completely naked and showing off my dick, but I think about the scars that sprawl all over my legs. They look like gnarly saplings with some skin. That's why I wear leggings as part of my outfit.

But here's the thing. I don't have a large dick and it doesn't get big when it's hard. I see other faeries prance about with their short dicks when they're soft, but I've seen them hard in the Love Canopy. I can see why they have nothing to be ashamed of. They've done the comparing thing, and they know they're A-OK in that department. That's what gives them the courage to strut about naked.

I bring all this up in our next heart circle. Even though it's not easy to do so, particularly because I want more than anything to be loved as I am, I look at each faerie in the eye as I share my concerns about the relative lack of sex in my life. It hurts when each one of them breaks eye contact with me. All 27 of them! It's like I can never win with even one person. Damn.

I had planned to remind them that I'm no different from them, but in the middle of my pointed outpouring, I forget. They are left with the bitter aftertaste of a crippled faerie's rant doled out with a carefully modulated voice.

Afterward, a few come up to me and whisper, "You're so brave."

The tone of their voices is patronizing. It's as if I'm supposed to be a child even though I'm 48 years old with a high-paying job. I don't point this out. Instead, I say, "Thank you."

In all honesty bravery had nothing to do with it. I thought that we were supposed to be as authentic as possible.

When I first heard of the faeries online, my first reaction was: why? Why would anyone want to sport a moustache, sprinkle glitter onto their pancake makeup, and strut around with a society lady's hat? They weren't drag queens trying to pass; if anything, they wanted to remind you that they were still men.

Yet there was something about them that drew my attention. In their world, there were no compartments. They strived to be whole within themselves. When I decided to try a heart circle that winter, I was relieved to find that it was held on the first floor in a house that had rainbow whirly-gigs spinning on its porch. Just a few steps, and I was in.

That evening I joined a circle of four other men. They regarded me with a look of equal interest and suspicion, but they did say hello. I never learned their legal names, but I learned they were Firehawk, Watusi Wasabi, Smurfina, and Jolly Fixins. They didn't look like what I thought faeries were supposed to look like: effeminate and equipped with a bitchy sense of humor. They looked quite bland with their clothes. Maybe it was just winter, and they needed to dress warm. As they took turns to share the deepest of their ongoing concerns, I came to see that they were human beings.

Of course, I'd known that we were all human beings, but until my first heart circle, I'd forgotten that simple fact about ourselves. I didn't have a faerie name then, but I knew I'd found something that I could call my own.

Every day at the retreat there's a workshop or two. I go to all of them. There's always something to learn from listening to others, but over the last few years I have been feeling antsy. This retreat hasn't been what I'd hoped it would be. There have been too many people, and most of them are young and genderqueer. I don't have a problem with young people, but I dislike it intensely when they treat me as if they have no connection with me whatsoever. I can see in their eyes that they're still feeling invincible from the rosy blush of their youth.

One of them is Pansy Fedora. He looks attractive in his own way: tall, clean-shaven, and baleful gray eyes. After having been among the faeries for the last ten years or so, I've come to recognize certain kinds of faeries like Pansy. They are the ones who'd felt like total misfits all their lives, so once they discover us, they get so into being faeries that they somehow feel entitled to be considered "experts" on the faerie experience even after only a few years. I love faeries, but those grand duchesses can be quite annoying. It's astonishing how some of them have already forgotten that the elders might have something equally valuable to contribute to the ongoing dialogues within our community. I just grit my teeth and say nothing, because their fervent evangelism will always drown me out no matter what I say. They don't seem to appreciate the fact that I, a faerie who's been one much longer than they have, have been willing to listen to their viewpoints.

This morning Pansy Fedora is giving a workshop about community building.

I go after my breakfast of honeyed tea and grapefruit. This should be interesting.

———

I'm sitting in the Big Tent where Pansy is giving his workshop. I listen to him lecture about the importance of connecting with each other through a number of shared activities, and I try not to roll my eyes. He's actually suggested a communal hike as an option, and I'm sitting right there in front of him. Has my flowery cane become invisible already?

I raise my hand. "It sounds all great, but what about faeries with disabilities? You need to remember that some of us can't walk as well as you."

He gives me a tight smile. "Well, like I said, it was only a suggestion."

"Exactly. If you weren't ableist, you'd have thought first whether an event was accessible before suggesting it. For instance, what if a wheelchair person wanted to join in? How would you—"

"It was only a suggestion!"

"Right." I glare at him. "You just don't get it, do you?" I lift my cane and slam it on the ground. "You've been talking about using activities based on the assumption that everyone will be able to get around easily. That's ableist privilege."

"Well, I'm sorry. That wasn't my intent."

"Good. Carry on."

He falters for the rest of the workshop. I can see the fear in his eyes that he'll offend me again. Good. He needs to be more mindful.

You see, I don't deal very well with bullshit. I'm just telling you as it is. If you don't like it, well, it's because you can't deal with the possibility of ending up like me one day.

Not all is dreary in my part of the world. The reason why I'm such a tough little broad is because of Hank Vernon. He was my first love.

He was an Iraq War veteran diagnosed with PTSD. He had nightmares that flashed on the insides of his eyelids when he dreamed, and he sometimes begged me to keep him awake as long as it was still dark outside. The tranquilizers didn't always help. His therapist suggested that I talk about everything but the war over there. When we talked about everything else, he was a magnificent angel.

We met in a hospital room. Isn't that funny? Me, on my last visit to the hospital. I was there for one last surgery, and I needed lots of pills to calm my nerves. God, I had come to hate doctors and nurses and surgeons by that point. Didn't matter if they were kind and compassionate. I simply had one botched operation too many over the course of my life. By then I had had seventeen surgeries on my legs. It got to the point when I involuntarily vomited each time before surgery. I hated being fixed over and over again. I couldn't understand why I had to be "repaired." I got along fine, I thought, but no, I wasn't walking right. Too much weight on my weak knee, so I had to have that fixed. Then my other knee gave out. It was as if my surgeon was a mechanic always tinkering with his dream car. I was a dream ongoing experiment. The pain in my legs throbbed so much I couldn't think of much else. I wanted morphine more than anything. The pain faded away, but my fear of hospitals never did.

When I woke up in the recovery room, I was alone. The same familiar grogginess that prodded me slowly out of anesthesia returned. I thought, *Hm. Morphine time.* The prospect filled me with the only kind of pleasantness I could find in these places. My mother was in the bathroom when a nurse came in to check on me. "Hello. Are you all right?" Her name ERIKA WOLK was engraved on her plastic badge pinned to her white dress. She gave me a smile as she searched into my eyes.

"Yeah," I said. "I'm ... water?"

As she poured some ice-filled water into a cup, I closed my eyes for a moment. I held the cup to my lips and looked at the door opened to the hallway. There, a handsome man with piercing blue eyes and a thick army jacket chanced to walk by, and in that moment, he simply stopped and looked at me. It was as if his entire soul was taking a single snapshot of my entire life. His eyes took in the pulleys that kept my knees in mid-air. He was honest with his curiosity.

All that day, as my mother hovered nearby, I prayed that he would return. I needed to stay there for a few more nights before I went home.

The next morning he did pop into my room. "How are you feeling?"

"Fabulous," I said.

He burst out laughing. "I hate these places, but I just had to." He paused. "I just had to see you."

I held up my hand. "Now you're seen."

We shook hands, and we couldn't stop talking and carrying on. It was wonderful. He confused my mother because I never had friends come by to visit, and he was a new friend? No matter.

It wasn't long before we were sixty-nining each other in my apartment. Beautiful cock. Perfect-sized for my mouth, really.

Weeks later, when the bandages came off my legs for good, he asked to see them. I didn't want to, but I was so in love with him, and at 25 I was feeling invincible. His reaction shocked me. He didn't turn away from my body completely naked there on the bed. He gazed at the crisscross of old and fresh scars that mapped all over my legs and whispered, "Fuck. That's so hot."

I didn't know what to say. I had heard of disability devotees before, but it wasn't until then I finally connected the dots around Hank. He had talked a lot about visiting his wounded army buddies in makeshift clinics out in the field, and how helpless he'd felt in wanting to take better care of them but couldn't because he was just another soldier.

He climbed onto my bed and knelt before me. I thought he was going to give me a blow job, but he tentatively licked all over my scars and moaned heavily as he jacked himself off. Aside from my mother, he was the first non-hospital person to explore the valley of my legs. I was grateful for his affections, but I didn't know what to make of them. I couldn't believe that anyone could develop a fetish for scars or deformed legs, but as long as I closed my mind to the idea that he was treating me as an object of his fantasies, I felt loved. He did give me everything that I hadn't known until that moment was due me. He gave me a lot of courage. He said I was worthy of having lots of friends. He held my hand on the sidewalk and stroked my thigh when we watched the Pride march together. He really didn't care about the looks we got when he leaned over and kissed me on the lips. He taught me the most important lesson that anyone ignored in this world needed to learn. I was worthy of love and so much more.

The beginning of the end of our lives together started with a simple comment when I put myself into a taxi before he closed the passenger door: "God, sometimes I wish you were in a wheelchair so I could help you out more."

"No," I said. "I prefer to be as independent as possible."

In our three years together we didn't have arguments or anything; we never fought. Ever.

That night our lovemaking took on a different tone, an unsteady rhythm. I had disappointed him, and he had disappointed me.

But in the end, it didn't really matter. The darkness came anyway.

Up until that frightening moment of his scream next to me, he had hidden the fact that he was taking a fair number of psychotropic drugs. I knew he was on antidepressants, which explained his occasional failure to get stiff, but I didn't begrudge him for that. He'd forgotten to pick up his meds for one or two days, and having him there wailing and crying and screaming in my arms frightened me. I was afraid his legs thrashing about would dislocate my knees, but by morning he calmed down.

I went through his stuff and saw how many pills he had to take. He wasn't suffering from just depression.

That night he ran naked out of our apartment, screaming incoherently about the Big Gun Eye aiming to kill us all. I tried to calm him down, but I couldn't keep up with him. He ran down the street and stopped the traffic at the intersection of Main and Johnson. The police had to be called in.

The next few years I had to overcome my fear of hospitals when I visited him every day in a psychiatric ward. Some days he looked and sounded coherent; then he looked absolutely frightened as a cat and needed to curl up in a corner somewhere. The emptiness next to me each night in bed made me cry.

When his psychiatrist conceded that there wasn't much else they could do but to keep him hospitalized for the foreseeable future, I cried.

I still visited Hank, but he eventually had become so medicated and blank-eyed that he didn't know who I was half the time.

I was so crushed. Weren't true loves supposed to recognized the spark in each other no matter what happened?

Eventually I had to tear myself away until I stopped going. The sleepless nights I got after each visit weren't just worth it. By then he had begun haunting my dreams. I didn't scream or anything. I just wanted to lie there on the bed and have him lick all that had made me ugly in the eyes of the world. I missed his tongue. I still do.

The older I become, the less patient I've become. I want to tell the retreat coordinators that they simply do not get it. Making the few rustic buildings fully wheelchair-accessible or hunting down an ASL interpreter for the lone Deaf faerie at the heart circle is only half the equation. People are the other half of the equation, and they are the ones who are so good at failing us freaks. It's time to stop the assumption that we freaks must always accommodate the able-bodied world. It's time that they be forced to think about our needs on a regular basis much like how we think about theirs.

Naturally they'll protest, "Nobody's perfect."

But what they don't realize is how much they live according to its corollary: "But most people will always be more perfect than you."

Of course, the able-bodied feel offended when I shame them, but they don't seem to understand that each of us freaks, especially with physical defects from a young age, have been shamed relentlessly all our lives. We are the ones who've been told from day one of diagnosis that we must change for their sake. They are not expected to change for our sake; it's their turf. We are the abnormal living in a world of normals, therefore we must eradicate the prefix "ab" from deep inside ourselves. It is our job to inspire the able-bodied community when we conquer the odds to be "normal" again. Of course, the great cosmic joke is that no one is ever normal, but no one is willing to concede to this fact. We are all closeted pervs. The sooner we remove the word "normal" from our vocabulary, the better off we will all be.

I'm so tired of explaining why they need to change their attitudes. I don't mind living with my knees for they are what they are, but I do mind having to explain myself over and over again. Can people be thoughtless? Yes. Sometimes I want to hit them on their heads with my cane.

You know what else I hate? The maxim that people use on fat women: "Someone will recognize you for the beautiful person you are inside." They say that physical beauty is ephemeral, but the beauty of soul is eternal. The trouble is, no one has eyes to enable them to see beyond the skin.

I want a man to love me as I am. I don't want to hear him say, "Maybe if you tried just one more surgical procedure, things would improve." I don't want to hear him say, "Is it okay if I dance with someone else?" I simply want to hear him say, "I love you because you're the most perfect man I've ever met."

Is that so hard for anyone to ask?

I often visit the Love Canopy early in the morning because the light is strong. I can see where I'm walking. Some tree roots that crisscross the path there are hard to climb over in the dark. Sometimes when I am alone in the Love Canopy, I jack off and imagine myself to be everyone's object of lust.

This morning the empty slings sigh slightly from a quiet wind. I am surprised to find Pansy naked and lying down on a blanket. He has been masturbating himself but with no passion. He looks startled when he realizes my presence.

"Sorry," I say.

"It's okay." He lets go of himself and sits up. "Wanna join me?"

I come closer. "Why all of a sudden?"

"Please."

"I don't want to be your pity fuck."

"No. It's just ..."

"I've seen guys like you pontificating about things they don't know shit about. That's why I had to speak up."

"I'm sorry."

I roll my eyes.

"What? I'm truly sorry!"

"Then change."

"What do you mean, change?"

"You didn't ask any of us to share *our* experiences with community building."

"Well, it's supposed to be a workshop."

"It wasn't a workshop. What you gave was a lecture. You can't have a lecture about community building and not have input from us."

"Well, sorry."

"Don't say that word anymore. Just *change*."

He looks at me. His eyes are bloodshot. "I thought maybe you ... we could ..." He points to himself.

"No," I say. "I don't want to be used to make you feel better about me."

He looks about himself. "I'm sorry." He gets up and leaves.

A moment later I detect the sound of a man crying. It's not loud, but as someone who used to cry himself to sleep, I'd know that sound anywhere.

Later that day I spot Pansy sitting at one end of the table in the cookhouse. He's been avoiding me all day. But it's dinnertime, and I must eat, and there's an empty space at the end of the other bench facing him. I sit right there in front of him. I scoop up a smattering of salad greens and drizzle vinaigrette all over it. I roll a steamed ear of corn onto my plate.

He averts his eyes as he eats.

I butter the ear.

He looks away when I pick up my corn and assiduously pick at the cob with my teeth. It feels like the longest meal of my life. I want so much to say something, but I have no idea how to start.

Bits of corn are wedged between my teeth.

I take a toothpick and scrape carefully.

He is still talking to others around the table and pretending that I'm not there.

When I am done with the toothpick and clearing my plate, the sky dims through the screened windows. Soon the dark invades our muted conversations around the table, and soon candles are lit.

I haven't said a word to anyone all evening.

I simply look at him. The fact that he's looking away from me tells me everything I need to know. He's ashamed of himself. He's not the first person I've shamed. I want to tell him that a well-intentioned heart will always be forgiven, but how do I tell him that without sounding remorseful?

When he catches me looking at him, I don't hide my feelings. I show him flickers of understanding, forgiveness, a pleading. I feel more naked than ever in my entire life.

I want to break down and cry, but I will not. I am stronger than this. I will show him that I do forgive him. I want to tell him that I understand what it feels like to be ashamed of not knowing any better. I want to hold him and tell him that he is a beautiful man. I want to turn the table over as if I'm a strongman, take off my shirt, and cushion my knees as I kneel before him and show him how a man can easily forgive another. Forgiving is easy, but being the first to forgive is the hardest thing in the world.

He still averts his eyes and talks quietly with Pandora Cox sitting next to him. They are talking about sharing the cost of gas when they drive together to Breitenbush next February. I want to tell them that I own a van that could easily accommodate six faeries or that I love to drive for hours on end. The road and I are best friends. Maybe it's because I'm never where I'm accepted, and there's a small hope deep inside me that if I get out on the road, I'll find that one place where I'll be loved as I am.

I still say nothing.

I am okay with this. I'm used to being seen as part of the scenery.

Finally, one candle after another flickers into the black.

Flashlights are turned on, and everyone murmurs good night as they leave the cookhouse and search for their tents out in the woods.

But he hasn't left.

We are alone.

"Hi," I say.

A moment passes. I can't see him very well. Just his silhouette created by the soft moon spreading its faerie dust outside.

"I'm so sorry. I didn't mean to—" A thickness catches in his voice.

"Hush. Give me your hand." I place my hand on the table.

He finds my hand, and I grip him. I slowly knead all over his hand for a long time. Could've been a minute or an hour. I can't tell. I am so into mining the core of himself through the subtle ways his hand responds to mine. The stiffness in his fingers evaporates. His breathing slows down. He is somehow not a human being; more of a shadow ready to break free of his body.

I don't say a word the entire time.

It's the sexiest thing I've ever done: this constant kneading while allowing all sorts of thoughts, both sexual and spiritual, to circulate throughout my body. I find myself erect.

My arms, having been stretched over the table, start to feel sore.

I give a deep sigh to warn him and let go.

But I am surprised when he grips my hands with his.

"My arms are sore."

I watch his shadow get up from the bench and walk around the table. He climbs over the bench next to me and takes my hands into his.

He massages my hands aggressively at first, but he eventually finds a rhythm that feels just right for us. My breathing soon matches his.

I close my eyes. As long as he touches me like this, I could sit like this forever.

Eventually he says, "Can you, um?"

"Um, what?"

I feel his arms reach forward and pull me into his arms. Even though he is a tall and lanky faerie, he feels surprisingly solid.

I am afraid to breathe. I am afraid to ask more, expect more. I have never felt this scared of anyone before.

Then he stifles a sob.

"It's okay, Pansy. I forgive you."

He starts to heave tears.

I too cry, but this time I pull him to my chest. I stroke his back. I think of swans moving gracefully across the water.

Our tears at last dried, he cradles my face and kisses me full on the lips.

I am stunned. It's not what you think it is, that because I'm disabled and therefore undesirable, I'd be content with the little crumbs of affection that fly my way. It's not that at all. It is how startlingly intimate we've become through our hands touching and needing each other. Even though I've heard the word "intimacy" many times, it feels suddenly new.

I respond with a kiss.

We taste each other's tongue.

His hands roam my chest, shoulders, back, and what little hair I have left on my head. I map him also.

His voice is thick with desire when he tries to speak: "How can I make it easier for you? Because I really ..."

I shush his lips with my finger. I am afraid he will say that he wants to apologize. I don't want him to break the spell that's overcome us. I hesitate. Walking in the dark is always a bad idea for me, and yet my cock needs him. I crave him worse than a man lost in the desert aching for a few drops of precious water. What should I say?

"Tomorrow."

"What?"

"I have to ..."

"Do you have a flashlight? I can take you to your tent."

Everyone knows that I have a huge tent. I don't do too well in tiny spaces, so it's easier for me to stand up and move around with my cane. "Okay."

He turns on his flashlight, and I turn on mine.

I hobble after him.

He is walking much slower than usual. Bless his heart.

Everything green looks oddly full of color in the crisp swaths of light crisscrossing in front of us. We hear the sound of crickets in the distance. I swat at the mosquitoes that try to nibble at my arms.

At my tent I unzip one flap. "You go in first." I step in right after him and zip up the tent. "Hold on." I zero my flashlight onto my unzipped sleeping bag. I don't tell anyone this, but it's always a struggle to zip my bag for the night by myself. That's why I prefer oversized bags. I'm afraid to break the magic that's lingering in the air between us, but I must.

"Do you want to stay the night?"

"I thought that was the general idea."

"Okay. I'll get into my bag, and you can ..."

"You want me to zip up after you? That's gonna be a challenge."

"No, you know what? I'll get in, and you zip me up. You just slide right in."

I take off my sandals and set down my cane when I push myself to my side of the sleeping bag. I am surprised to see that he is taking off all his clothes.

He catches the look on my face. "Is this okay?"

"Yeah," I smile. "You look beautiful."

He seems oddly shy when he discards his underwear.

He is about to zip me up when I say, "Wait." I sit up and pull off my toga. I am totally naked except for the leggings. "I'm ready."

He zips me up.

He angles himself with his backside to me when he tries to snuggle down into our cocoon. I am afraid to touch his body even when he is fully against mine. He turns off the flashlight. As he turns around, we negotiate our arms and legs until we meld.

Our cocks touch as we press fiercely against each other.

We grind.

We kiss.

Our grinding is endless like the sea.

Then—our bodies quake. We grip each other.

We don't say a word. Our gasps have enough language.

Our sticky bodies whisper to each other as if they are negotiating a truce behind closed curtains.

We fall asleep without learning the agreed-upon terms.

It is mid-morning when we at last awaken.

"Hello, gorgeous," I say.

"Oh, hi there." He gives me a kiss.

We cuddle for a bit.

"I gotta pee," he finally says. He pushes himself out of our sleeping bag and leaves the tent. I hear the sound of his urine splashing against a tree nearby.

When he returns, he says, "Are you hungry?"

"Yeah, but ..." I pat the empty space next to me.

He surprises me when he unzips our bag and spreads it apart. He reclines against me and looks at my warped legs for a long moment. "Can I see your, um?"

I know what he wants to see. I am a car accident waiting to be rubbernecked. I sit up and pull down the leggings. This is a make-or-break moment. Soon he will see how ugly like tree bark my legs are, and he will lose all desire for me, and he will apologize for what happened last night, saying that he didn't know what he was doing. The usual excuses. I avert my eyes from his face.

He says. "I thought they would look worse than that."

I turn to him. "Oh, thank you!"

I am stunned to see him smiling so awkwardly. I know that expression too well. It means that he's crossed a line where society had expected him not to compliment someone who is supposed to be ugly.

141

He plumbs the depth of my eyes with his own. I notice they are brown as chocolate.

He says, "Tell me about community building."

I smile. "First, you hold a man's hand for the longest time and tell him, without saying a word, how much you want to understand him."

He moves closer to my body and grips my hands. "Tell me again."

For the first time in my life, I'm too happy to say absolutely nothing.